AF579787

ANGELS IN DISGUISES

Sita Bietz, Laura Singh and Deo Ramlal. I've been through many ups and downs in recent times but through it all, you guys were always just one call away. Thanks for your tenacious push and support. Truly appreciate you guys.

SECRET

DESIRES

VALENTINA DIMITRI

MYSTICAL PUBLISHING
&
CONSULTATION SERVICES

Mystical Publishing & Consultation Services

mysticalpublishing777@gmail.com

ISBN: 978-976-97271-1-3

Publishers Note

Trinidad and Tobago

CHAPTER ONE

"Look at all these bills, John. How are they going to get paid?" Caroline shouted, slamming the stack of bills to the floor. She stretched her hands out before placing them back on her hips.

Caroline paced the white tiled floor of the living room. "We're already in arrears. Been like that for the past two months, John!" She approached him, lifting both hands into the air as she screamed again.

"Don't you think you're overreacting just a bit?" John responded to his wife's ranting.

The calm, collective manner in which he spoke annoyed Caroline even more. "Overreacting! You say. I worked my ass off!" She tilted her head back. "I've been working a double shift for two damn months, John. I barely slept, hardly finding the time to eat. Hell! I can't even remember the last time I slept on my bed in the comfort of my darn house. Do you even know what that's like? Of course not!" She muttered beneath her breath, shaking her head in disbelief at how inconsiderate the man she married could be. "You wouldn't... You were too busy drinking and gambling the little I worked my ass off for you even to care." She answered herself, not wanting a response from him.

John walked with long strides between the two grey walls that led him into the kitchen, getting himself a bottle of whiskey and a glass. "There's always something or the other with you, right? I wouldn't say I like the nagging, Caroline. Yet, it's all you ever seem to do: *nag, nag, nag...*"

"Well!" Caroline took a deep, prolonged breath, her cheek flushed. "Forgave me for being the only one concerned about whether or not this will be the last month or week we'll have a roof over our heads. Or the luxury and comfort of a bed to sleep on." She gritted her teeth with a feeling that she was not getting through to him, and neither did he fully understand the seriousness of the situation that they were in.

Pouring some whiskey into a glass, John strolled back towards the living room area, again peering at the grey walls. (*He couldn't help thinking how well the dull color matched his life perfectly.)* "I don't see what the big deal is. Everyone makes mistakes, Caroline... I'm not the first, and I won't be the last. Besides, I can always put in extra work hours, and so can you. Things will work out. They always do."

"Have you lost your God damn mind!" she shouted; the glass of whiskey went flying across the room, followed by shattered pieces of glass. "Have you been listening to anything I've said, John? Have you ever noticed your wife wasn't in bed for the past couple of months?" She gritted her teeth, and tension riddled her voice.

"What the fuck! Caroline," John yelled, clenching his fist into a ball; he lifted his hand briefly but quickly lowered it back to his side, taking a deep, prolonged breath.

"Put in extra hours! That's a laugh. Tell me, John. When was the last time you did a day's work? Do you even remember the last time you went to the office? Because I sure as hell can't!" She glared at his clenched fingers. She was daring him to lay a hand on her.

"You're lucky Logan hasn't fired your ass! Cause, honestly, I can't understand how you got him to put up with a piece of crap like you for this long. Two months, John!" She pounds her fist on the table.

"Two darn months! Sleepless nights, working my fingers to the bone. How John? Please explain to me how what took me months to save took you one night to lose?" Pressing her fingers to her throbbing forehead.

"Come on, Caroline, calm yourself down..." Reaching out, John massaged her shoulders. "I'm sorry, Hun." He lifted her chin. "I'll make this up to you. I promise?"

"I'm tired, John." Caroline sigh. "I don't know how long I can continue doing this."

"Tired of what, Caroline?" John asked. "What are you trying to tell me?" he sounded slightly annoyed and unpleased at her proclamation.

Caroline slumped into the sofa. "I've been trying, John. But this is all getting too much for me now." She looked up at John, finding it hard to hold back the tears that filled her eyes and streamed down her cheeks like an overflowing river.

"I've already apologized, Caroline. What else do you want from me?" he exasperated, feeling a sudden heat rushing throughout his entire body.

"I'm afraid sorry isn't going to pay our bills, John. Nor will it guarantee a roof over our heads!" She retorted much to match his tone. Raising from the worn-out old sofa, she scampered past him into the kitchen, emptying every bottle of alcohol she could put her hands on into the kitchen sink.

"What the hell! Have you gone mad?" John rushed over, tugging at the bottles.

"What does it matter, John?" She shoved him to the side, sobbing hysterically.

"Won't you the one just saying things will get better?" Wiping her tear-soaked face on her sleeves. "If that's the case, then you shouldn't miss these now, should you?"

"You're a fucking psychopath!" John grabbed her by the throat, pushing her against the sink. He began squeezing, choking her. Caroline could feel the air sucking out of her body. She wrestled with him, trying to free herself, clawing across his face.

"Why, you little bitch!" John shouted out, feeling a sharp, burning pain across his face. He threw Caroline against the wall. Wiping his cheek, he stared at his blood-stained fingers. The red substance seemed to have made him even more aggressive. Walking towards her, he leaned forward, grabbing her by the throat again. He dealt her two slaps on each side of her face.

"Why do you always make me do this to you?" He screamed out. "Fuck this! You're not worth the jail time!"

Caroline slumped forward, sliding to the floor. Her body was much too weak at this point to hold herself up.

"I need a fucking drink!" he vented, slamming the door behind him as he stormed off.

Struggling, Caroline dragged herself against the wall. Huddling her knees towards her chest, she broke down. Allowing her tears to flow, for she knew deep inside she would not be able to hold it together for much longer. Once, too many times, she had allowed this to happen. Once too many times, she had forgiven John.

He will return home later tonight or maybe even in the wee hours of the morning, whichever suits him. He'll reek of alcohol, *confessing how sorry he was and had no idea what got over him.* John will beg her forgiveness, and naïve as she was, she always did.

John had taken so much from her in their five years together as husband and wife. He was not to be blamed alone, for she had allowed him that power over her. She was head over heels and foolishly in love with her husband that nothing he did, in her eyes, could ever be wrong.

The ringing phone propelled Caroline's trembling hands upwards, forcing her to reach for the cell phone on the small round kitchen table.

"Maranda," As much as Caroline missed her best friend, there was no way she could answer her call. Maranda would instantly pick up that something was not right. (*She was that good*) It had been so very long since their last conversation. John had ensured that, forbidding her from having further contact with Maranda. Not long after, doing the same with everyone she held near and dear to her heart, keeping her in isolation for none other than his selfish reasons.

Caroline got to her feet reluctantly, in no mood for company. Stopping briefly to look at her appearance in the wall mirror, she fixed herself up a bit before she strode towards the front door, getting even more annoyed as the doorbell rang again for the third time and then forth.

"Be right there!" Caroline yelled, picking her pace up a bit. She reached for the door handle.

"Maranda..." The name barely escaped Caroline's lips. She stood hugging the door for support. "You're the last person I expected to see here." She said. Fumbling with her words.

"Well, there won't be any answer to your calls, Caroline. I've been trying to get through with you for over a week." The woman walked past Caroline into the kitchen, with Caroline almost running behind to keep up. Turning the stove on, Maranda filled the kettle, placing it on the burner. Folding her arms, she leaned back against the kitchen sink.

"You look like you've seen better days." Maranda examined Caroline from the head down and back up again. "Tell me... How has life been treating you?" A worried and concerned look across her face at the sight of her friend. She wished she had heeded her brother's advice to visit and check in on Caroline sooner.

"Things have been good. No complaints." Caroline shook her head, forcing a smile. Pulling out a bar stool from the grey island marble kitchen counter, she climbed up, making herself comfortable.

"Hum, I see." Maranda took two steps. Tiptoeing, she opened the cupboard on the left side of the kitchen sink. "Now let's see, if my memory serves me correctly, ah... yes, here they are." She took two white coffee cups out, bustling around the kitchen.

An awkward silence filled the room for a moment.

"Here you go." Passing a cup of steaming, hot coffee over to Caroline. "Black a little milk, no sugar." She winked at Caroline with a bright and enthusiastic smile written on her face.

Caroline watched as the steam eagerly escaped its way through the mouth of the coffee mug. Reaching her hands forward. "You remembered?" A genuine smile curved her lips.

"It's what friends who care for each other do, Hun." Maranda climbed onto one of the bar stools, blowing gently into her coffee before allowing herself a small sip while observing her friend over the rim of her cup.

One of the first things she noticed was the blue, black marks on Caroline's face. Secondly were the ones around her neck. Her not-so-well attempts to conceal them weren't working well in her favor. The fact that Caroline kept pulling her hair forward and around her shoulders only drew even more attention to her while at the same time telling Maranda that if she were to help her friend get out of this marriage. She would need to approach this situation gently and with much precaution.

She could not afford to alienate Caroline more than she already was. She remembered what had occurred a few months earlier when John had made the mistake of slapping Caroline in her present. This ended in a much-heated argument, leaving John with a broken nose and swollen lips.

(*"Maybe the next time you'll think twice about doing something like that again.)* Maranda screamed at John with raging eyes and heavy breathing after using her martial arts skills on him. She knew she was only supposed to use this skill in self-defense. This was one of the first things they trained when the classes were signed up for. But she figured this situation called for it. (*Besides, the son of a bitch deserved what he got, and honestly, he was lucky his balls were still in place when she was finished with him that evening.)*

Either way... Maranda would not sit idle and watch a man abuse her friend that way. (*Not in front of her, that is*). There was no way she would have it happening to any woman... It was never in her nature to watch a woman being taken advantage of and disregarded.

However, Maranda lost something she held dear to her heart then. Caroline and her friendship had broken off, forcing her to decide between herself and John. Caroline chose her husband, of course. (*I mean, which woman would not have? So, Maranda did not entirely* blame Caroline when she did so.)

Trembling and with tears streaming down her face that said night, Caroline turned to her and asked that she leave.

"*Are you sure this is what you want*?" Maranda remembered her words as vividly as though it had happened yesterday.

"Yes, it is." The words escaped Caroline's trembling lips.

Broken and hurt, Maranda left that evening, walking away from her and Caroline's twenty-year friendship. Had it not been for a recurring dream and Logan's persistence, she probably would not have been here today.

However, she scrutinized Caroline again, no longer questioning her decision to show up at her friend's doorstep unannounced.

"Look, Maranda," Caroline spoke, breaking the awkward silence that filtered the small grey and white kitchen area.

"I'm sorry for how I treated you; I can only hope someday you'll find it in your heart to forgive me and maybe even forget what I did to you."

"Forget what?" Maranda gave her friend a playful, childlike look, trying to break this unknown heaviness that filled the air.

Caroline glared at Maranda, finding it much too painful to smile through her blood-shut, watery eyes.

"I missed you so much." The words filtered out of Caroline's mouth before she realized they did so.

"I know, Hun." Maranda jumped off her bar stool, placing her arms around Caroline in the most comforting way. "Truth be told, I missed you more." Wiping the stream of tears that ran down her friend's cheeks

"Don't cry, Caroline. Please, it's not that bad." Pushing Caroline's hair backward. Exposing her neckline, the blue and black bruises throughout Caroline's body were evident enough. "I should have been here." Maranda hugged her friend again, being gentle enough not to hurt her more than she already was. "I need to get you to the hospital."

"No!" Scampering off her chair. "No hospitals!" Caroline paced in the small room in a fidgety state. "Please..." Pleading with Maranda.

"Okay, calm down. No hospital." Maranda promised, realizing she had pushed Caroline a little too quickly. "I should have insisted you come with me that night; I should never have left you with that coward that calls himself a man." Maranda's heart rapidly pounded in her chest, grateful that John was not around, for there was no telling what she could do to him now.

"I am as much to be blamed as the son of a bitch, himself." Suddenly, feeling a combination of guilt and anger at the same time. "What kind of a friend would just leave like that," Maranda asked. Her question was meant more for herself than Caroline.

"It's not your fault, Maranda. I was the one who pushed you away, or have you forgotten? You did nothing wrong." Caroline sniffled into a heap of napkins, holding a few out to Maranda. "I know why I'm crying, but why are you?" Caroline asked carelessly, wiping her already red nose.

"Because it hurts me when you hurt," Maranda murmured, wiping her wet face. "Come, grab your coffee. Let's walk out to the balcony. I think we both could do with a bit of fresh air."

CHAPTER TWO

Maranda observed Caroline leaning against the white railings on the balcony overlooking their beachfront property. She was lost in her thoughts as she sipped on her probably cold coffee by now.

"I love this place. One can easily get lost in this world." Smiling to herself as the wind wiped her hair across her face. "It's so peaceful out here. It'll hurt me if I should lose any of it after so many years. Do you know this was my grandmother's and her mother's before that?"

"Care to tell me what happened?" Maranda walked over, took the empty cup from Caroline's hand, and placed it on the white patio beside them. "I'm here for you, Hun." Taking both Caroline's hands in hers. "I promise that no matter what happens in the future, no one will ever get in between our friendship, not ever again."

A small smile curved Caroline's lip. "Thanks, Maranda. It means a lot hearing you say that. I don't know how I ever got along all those months without you."

"Oh, that's easy, you couldn't." Maranda waved her fingers out front laughing.

"You haven't changed one bit, Maranda." Caroline laughed, not remembering the last time she felt this relaxed. "We have much catching up to do, don't we? Tell me, how have you been keeping yourself? And how is Logan?"

"Still crazy over you, if that's what you're asking?" Maranda smiled, observing how Caroline lit up at mentioning Logan's name.

"I asked no such thing." Caroline babbled; her cheeks flushed pink. Turning away, she hoped Maranda had not noticed. "Has he ever asked for me, I mean?"

"I know what you mean. And yes, all the time." Caroline had always smitten Logan, and at one point, Maranda thought the affection would have been returned. Sadly, it was not to be as soon after John came into town sweeping Caroline off her feet.

It broke Logan's heart to watch the woman he loved walk down the aisles with his best friend. However, try as he may over the years, he could not get Caroline or his feelings for her out of his mind, enquiring about her every chance he got but keeping his distance simultaneously. Caroline was her brother's one weakness, but destiny had played a cruel game with them both.

Deciding it was best to lead the subject away from Logan for the time being. "So now that we got Logan out of the way. Tell me, what's this about you losing the house?" Maranda asked, a bit confused as to what was going on.

"I received a letter from the bank this morning." Caroline's eyes drifted to the floor.

"And?" Maranda eagerly pursued.

"And... John has been collecting and hiding the mail for a while now. The letter stated that we had six weeks to pay or face the consequence of being evicted."

Maranda stared at Caroline. "You mean you guys could lose this house?" a flabbergasted look covered her face.

"I'm afraid so." Caroline nodded.

"I don't understand, but why? How did you allow this to happen?" Maranda asked... I thought you were up to date with all the payments.

"My darling husband has not been paying our mortgage all this time." Caroline turned and stared aimlessly at the ocean view that overlooked the balcony.

Maranda stepped before Caroline, bringing her attention back to their conversation. "What do you mean he hasn't been paying the mortgage? Isn't that why Logan decided to keep John's name on the payroll, even after his screw-up?"

"Logan?" Caroline's eyes swiftly reverted to Maranda's. "What does Logan have to do with this? And what do you mean, kept John's name on the payroll? I don't understand?" she says, staring at Maranda. Her eyes were riddled with confusion.

Caroline's questions baffled Maranda. "You don't know... Do you?" Maranda asked. "Why doesn't any of this surprise me?" Maranda asked.

"Know what? What are you talking about?" Caroline enquired impatiently.

"Son of a bitch!" Maranda peered at her friend. "He hasn't told you, has he?"

"Tell me what, Maranda. You're speaking in puzzles here?" Caroline did not like where this was going but needed to know simultaneously.

"John lost his job almost three months back, Caroline. He came to work drunk one morning and screwed up some paperwork that cost the company millions. Logan completely lost it. He didn't fire John. But he told him to take some time off while at the same time advising John to get his act together or risk losing everything. However, He suspended him with half his pay, hoping he would eventually come to his senses.

"That's why John hasn't been going to the office," Caroline muttered more to herself than Maranda. "Logan should have fired his ass instead."

"Oh boy..." Maranda looked at the gold band wristwatch in her left hand.

"Look at the time already. I really must get going." Maranda hassled indoors.

"Oh no, you don't." Caroline rushed after her friend.

"Something is going on here, and you, Missy. Are not leaving until you tell me what it is!" Grabbing Maranda's arms roughly.

"My, my... now that's what I like to see. Aren't you an aggressive one?" Maranda looked down at Caroline's fingers, still digging into her upper arm. "Now, Darling, that's exactly the kind of wildcat I want to see if and when your good-for-nothing husband ever tries anything like this on you again. Comprehend me." Maranda gently tugged her hand from Caroline's grip.

"Maranda!" Caroline please,

As much as she liked this aggressive side of her friend because, to her, it meant Caroline had finally had enough and was finding the strength to stand up for herself. "I can't, Caroline. I'm sorry, but I have to go now. I've already said more than I should."

"And who's going to know?" Caroline folded her arm across her chest and gazed at her friend.

Maranda shook her head with a smug smile painted across her face. "Touché! My, you are getting good at this bitchy thing, aren't you? I like it, but I have not mentioned it to you. Logan is going to kill me if he finds out."

"Logan?" Caroline squinted her eyes, tilting her head to the side. "What does Logan have to do with all this, Maranda?"

"Nothing, and yet everything..."

"Okay, now I'm confused." Caroline didn't have a clue what was going on. But the more she found out, the more questions it left her with.

"I know you don't understand... You couldn't, just that it's not my place to squeal."

"Then help me to understand." Rudely cutting across her friend.

Maranda slides her jacket on, lifting her long black hair. She allowed it to fall loosely across her back. Leaning forward, she picked her handbag up from the sofa where she had carelessly thrown it earlier in her haste. “You want answers, Caroline?”

“Please?”

“Then speak with Logan,” she gave her friend a slight nod of approval.

“Not this again.” throwing a small tantrum. “How many times have I told you, Maranda? I’m not in the least bit interested in your brother.”

“You know what they say. Actions speak louder than words, sweetheart.” Maranda briskly walked towards the door. “I have to go now, Hun. Got an appointment for eleven-thirty.” Turning to give her friend offering a warm hug.

“Meet with Logan, Caroline. Please… I promise you’ll get the answers you’re looking for.” A light peck on the cheek and a wave of goodbye. Caroline watched Maranda skip the three steps like a playful child before jumping into her red Toyota Hatchback. With a wave of goodbye, Maranda blew a kiss on Caroline’s way before pulling her car onto the road and disappearing down the busy streets.

Shutting the door behind her, Caroline wondered what Maranda was babbling about as she ensured the door leading to the balcony was secured and locked before making her way up the staircase toward her bedroom. While unanswered questions plagued her mind, Caroline couldn’t help but wonder if this was another one of Maranda’s many attempts to get her and Logan together.

Caroline couldn’t quite place her finger on precisely what it was, but something about Maranda’s visit had her thinking—elated as she was to see her best friend standing at her doorsteps this morning. *She couldn’t help but wonder why the unexpected visit. Why now, and what was the real reason behind it?*

Peeling her clothes off, Caroline climbed into the shower, washing the unwanted memories of yet another day away. Shutting her eyes tightly, she allowed the sprinkles of rain-like drops to clean her tears away like so many times before today.

She had gotten so tired over the past years. Tired of the fighting, tired of crying, tired of trying to hold it all together while she was slowly falling apart inside, she found that she was tired of life itself.

CHAPTER THREE

Logan's eyes travelled across the room to the beautiful, enchanting woman walking toward their table. Her silver high heels matched perfectly with a long navy-blue evening dress that dragged behind her, exposing her lovely long legs with each step that conveyed her closer. Her broad hips swayed elegantly from side to side. Her attire highlighted her emerald green eyes that seemed to sparkle with the bright chandelier lights.

How he would have loved to bury his nose into those lovely black curls hanging loosely over her shoulders that hid *most of her cleavage. A pity, he thought silently. She belonged to a man who had never appreciated what he had.* Nonetheless though. She carried herself well, being the envy of almost every female. In contrast, men lust after her.

Drawing closer to the table, Logan couldn't help noticing the tiny pink of Caroline's tongue as it slowly glided across her lips. Instantly feeling the awakening of his not-so-well-trained cock. Shifting a little in his chair, Logan was only too triumphant, at least for the camouflage of the dark, brown-painted table top. Reaching his hand beneath the table, he adjusted his crutch.

"*My wife's a beauty, isn't she?*" John's voice intruded on Logan like a cold shower, bringing his musing back to the table and their current situation.

Logan cast a glance at Caroline once more. Then he focused on the three men sitting around the table before throwing his cards in, conceding.

"Cut your losses and go home with your wife, John. I draw the line at taking a man's house away from his family."

"Then you should take her," John said with glee, tilting his head toward Caroline.

John's words gained the full attention of Henry, a short, bald, shabby-looking man who sat at the head of the table. "A tempting bet, John. I must say, she is indeed a beauty. But I'm with Logan on this one. There's something called ethics. I just so happen to live by it. Besides, Lara Lee will kill me, should she come to find out." throwing his cards on the table. "I'm out as well." He pushed his chair backward, removing himself from the game.

Logan stared at John with an appalled look, in disbelief over what he had heard. "This has to be another one of your jokes, right?" he inquired.

"Why hate the player, man? Hate the game." John said. They assured Logan that he meant every word he said.

"Have you lost your damn mind, John?

"Come on, Logan. Don't play naïve with me. I've seen how you look at my wife. The way you've always looked at her, even a blind man would take notice." He signaled for the dealer to start the game. "This is your one chance to make that dream a reality." John winked at Logan. "One night, I'm giving you the opportunity of a lifetime, man." He spread his arms out with a smug grin that curved his lips from ear to ear. "You should be thanking me, my friend." He continued with an arrogant, self-righteous look.

His obnoxious laugh has never annoyed Logan as much as it did tonight.

"Deal me in." Amir, one of the town's divorcees, pulled a chair out and made himself comfortable. He rubbed the palms of his hands together with a devilish look. Lowering his eyes, he glared sideways at Caroline.

Logan could only imagine his thoughts where Caroline was concerned. Amir was married to Karen, one of Logan's cousins. However, their marriage was short-lived. After only a year and nine months, Karen came home early from work one day to meet her husband in bed with one of the town slut Clair. Logan remembered the day as though it was yesterday.

Karen came to his house sobbing uncontrollably and wondering where she had gone wrong and what she could have done differently. Try as he may to convince her that none of it was her fault. She blamed herself for returning to her husband a mere two weeks later. Where at first, everything seemed fine until three months down the road. The very same scenario repeated itself again and then again.

Logan watched as his once happy, cheerful, vibrant cousin turned into someone dejected and hateful, lashing out at the world around her.

Karen and Amir's lives continued until Karen had had enough. They were finding the courage and strength within. She left their house, serving Amir Divorce papers six weeks later.

Not long after their divorce was finalized, Karen packed up, leaving town. So yes, it's no secret that Amir was one of Logan's least favorite people worldwide.

"This should be very interesting." Amir eagerly awaited the game to get started.

Logan stared at Amir. He hasn't changed one bit. He was still the same egotistical, conceited, arrogant, self-centered bastard he always was. Not realizing his words were spoken out loud.

"Come on, Logan. Don't be a spoiled sport. Let's give the guy a chance." John's arrogance once again interrupted Logan's thoughts.

"My God! John, you are serious about this?" Logan leaned forward, slamming his fist on the table. "John, she's your wife, man!" His teeth clenched together, tightening his jaw as he spoke. "Not some piece of trash you picked up at the side of the road." pushing the cards back towards John. "Let's say we forget this happened, and I take you guys home."

The three men seemed to have pulled an even bigger crowd as everyone gathered around their table, curious about the outcome of this game and its stakes.

"Never figured you to be a coward," cast Logan a warning sign as Caroline approached the table.

"Hate to spoil your fun, but John, dear, you promised one more game an hour ago. Can we leave now, please?" She sighs in utter frustration. An apprehensive, fidgety feeling took over as she was the center of attention when all eyes were suddenly focused in her direction.

"You still have time to change your mind, John." Secretly hoping in his mind that his friend would not. Spending a night in sweet ecstasy with Caroline would be a night to remember forever. Logan had been dreaming of it ever since he looked at her, so why should he not take the chance now that it was offered to him? After all, if John was her husband and he didn't care, why should he be the one to feel guilty? And besides, he couldn't stand the thought of Caroline being in the arms of any man, much less Amir.

He tried to convince himself that he was doing this in Caroline's best interest; he knew deep inside that it was also for his egotistic reasons.

Logan shifted in his chair, moving forward. He reached out, lifting the edge of the two cards dealt to him, peeping under. An ace and a king of hearts. He looks at the three cards on the table from beneath his eyelids, Jack and Ten of Hearts with a queen of spades. Something could happen here, thinking silently, not wanting to give himself away.

Leaning back in his chair, Logan held his composure, rubbing his right index finger beneath his lips, casting a sideward glance at Amir.

He seemed a bit tense. This was a good sign. It meant that he had nothing to worry about where Amir was concerned. Logan then focused his undivided attention on John, whose smug smile gave him away. He told Logan he was dealt a firm hand based on his years of experience playing the game.

Aside from the soft melody of Kenny G's instrumental music that echoed throughout the room. An awkward quietness took over as tension in the game built. Everyone fought to get a closer look, wanting to be the first to see what the outcome of this game would be.

Caroline looked at the crowd surrounding the table, then at her husband with a demented look. Every pore in her body raised, telling her something was wrong. “What is going on, John?” The panic in her voice was not well hidden. “What is Logan speaking about? Change of mind. For what?” raising her voice to gain her husband’s attention.

Maranda took Caroline’s hand, whispering into her ear.

“He did what!” Caroline could feel the color drained from her face. Her knees shook so severely that she held on to Maranda’s shoulder.

“You’re worrying your pretty little head about nothing, darling?” he patted her on the ass, paying her no natural mind, turning his attention back to the table and the game as the dealer turned over the last two cards—queen of hearts with five clubs.

Logan sat back quietly, looking at the queen of hearts that was turned up on the table.

Amir threw his hands in folding. “Looks like I’m out.” Amir stood up. “Well, everyone, I can’t say it hasn’t been fun. I look forward to the next bet, John.” He winked at Logan, refusing to relinquish his manly ego as he conceded.

“Too bad, Logan. Would have been a night for you to remember.” Turning the two tens, he was dealt with upright on the table. “A ten house.” John happily announced with a smirk in triumph. “See, darling. You had nothing to worry about.”

Frozen, Caroline stood staring down at her husband. How could a man be this heartless? Even as she stood witnessing what was happening, her mind still refused to believe it. This man was her husband. After all, he promised to love and protect her, shutting her eyes tightly. Someone, please wake me up from this dream. Opening her eyes again only to realize it was no dream but an absolute live nightmare, a single tear ran down her cheek.

Logan sat reclined in his chair with a finger beneath his chin, observing his friend for a few seconds more. This man had no regrets over what he had just done. He held no remorse for what he was doing. Reaching forward, Logan slowly started to turn his cards over individually.

"Ten... Jack... Queen... King and Ace of Hearts." He took his time in calling the cards out. "A royal flush!" Logan announces.

John looked on in disbelief, shocked at what he was seeing.

Logan took no joy in teaching his friend this lesson, but it had to be learned. And from where he stood, it was best known from him than anyone else.

"What can I say, man." John laughed out loud. "All is fair in the game of love, wouldn't you say."

It was clear to Logan that John did not intend to admit that what he did was wrong. Pushing his chair backward, Logan stood up, straightening his tie. He looked at John. "I truly feel sorry for you, man... You disgust me, and I mean that in the most distasteful way possible."

He was clearing his way through the crowd surrounding the table, still dismayed. Logan stood for a brief moment, not turning around. "I'll be at my apartment, John. Don't keep me waiting too long." His voice was stern and held no compassion. "I'm very impatient, but I guess you already knew that." He said before walking towards the exit of the nightclub.

This was John's burden to carry. Logan stood before Angels of The Night Club, squinting his eyes as he blew out another puff of smoke from his lungs. Taking another long drag from his cigar, he flipped the butt to the ground pressing his feet over it, rotating, before climbing into his silver Toyota 4by4 Hilux van. He drove off in the direction of his apartment to prepare for the arrival of his guest.

CHAPTER FOUR

"Come on, Caroline, don't be like this." John poured the last of the whiskey from the bottle into his glass.

Caroline's hand lifted before she realized what she had done, feeling the burning of her palms against John's cheek. "Bastard!" Her eyes were blood-shut red and filled with tears that ran profusely down her face.

John lifted his hand, rubbing his cheek, twisting his jaw from side to side. "I'd let that slide." He calmly responded. "Accepting that I was wrong and I did go overbroad a wee bit tonight, a minor mistake, Caroline. Anyone could have made it. I'll blame the alcohol if it makes you feel better." Holding the empty bottle out front.

Caroline's teeth clenched with the force of her hand against John's face for the second time.

"What the hell, Caroline?" grabbing at the table edge, trying to regain his balance.

"Mistake?" She yelled, hearing her voice echoing as it bounced around throughout the vast conference room owned by Mr Morgan. He was kind enough to offer them. While simultaneously trying to protect Caroline from the contemptuous glares and attitude of the nosey crowd that stood outside shamelessly awaiting the verdict.

"Forgetting to pick me up after work was an inaccuracy. Reversing the darn car into a brick wall was an inaccuracy. Fucking, Clair was a huge blunder, John!" she gritted her teeth. "Gambling your wife?" She inhaled deeply, feeling the rise and fall of her uncontrollable breathing, glaring at her husband with utter and pure contempt.

Caroline felt a sudden throbbing pounding in her forehead as she fought to calm herself while simultaneously trying to regain control of her emotions. "What kind of a man would even do that to his wife, John?" She looked away, unable to control her tears nor the quivering of her bottom lips.

"Did you even stop to think, just once? Even for a moment, what was this going to do to me? Do to us? Did I mean that little to you, John? After all these years, was our marriage terrible that you would give me away as though I were nothing to you but a piece of old jewelry?" The tears streamed down her cheek. Caroline grabbed a few napkins from the huge round table in the center of the large room.

(Get a grip on yourself, Caroline. This man has already taken so much away from you... He has stripped you of literally everything. And tonight... Your dignity. Please don't give him the satisfaction of seeing you fall apart. At least you still have your pride. Walk away with it.) The voices in her head taunt her.

"Caroline, Honey..." John reached forward.

"Don't touch me!" She flinched, pulling her hands away from him. "Don't you ever, dear, touch me again!" Her yells could be heard above the loud music outside their door.

Morgan looked over to the DJ, nodding and signaling for him to turn the music a nudge.

"You know what, John." Slowly sliding the wedding ring off her finger. "After what you did tonight! There's nothing left between us. This marriage is over, John. You made darn sure of that tonight.

"Come on, Caroline. Don't do this." Staring at the gold band that Caroline so callously threw on the table. "Don't you think you're taking this too far? I promise I'll change this time."

With a half-suppressed, scornful laugh, Caroline glared at John beneath her brows. "I'm taking it too far, John?" For a moment, she could not believe those words had come out of his mouth. "Are you even listening to yourself?" Her gaze locked into his as she closed the gap between them. Never in her entire life had she ever felt this much contempt towards any one person before tonight, and for this reason, she seemed highly grateful. For it gave her the strength, she needed to do something she should have done long ago. "You know what, John?" Feeling no need to justify herself to him anymore.

"Since I'm the one that's taking it too far. I'll take it a little bit further. I'm going over to Logan's apartment. I'm going to fuck Logan, John." Taking extreme pleasure in the way, John squirmed as the twitching of his jaw line was highly noticeable, and the clenching of his fist gave her the satisfaction she sought in avenging him for what he had done to her.

"I'm going to fuck him hard, John. I'm going to fuck Logan, however, and wherever he wants to slide his hard cock into me. On the sofa, on the bed, in the shower, we might even try it against the wall. Oh, and you know how I love being pinned against the wall with my ass pushed back while feeling the roughness of a rock-hard cock sliding into my wet, slimy pussy."

She paused for a bit, reveling in John's despair. She moistens her dry lips, tormenting him that much further. Her only mission at this point is revenge. "I'm getting wet just thinking about this." She continued, still not through with her spiteful intent.

"I'm going to enjoy doing Logan, John. And don't worry about a thing, Darling, I'll be sure to give him his money's worth. Oops!" placing her hand to her mouth. "I really should be choosing my words wisely. Your money's worth."

For a brief moment, she saw what she had never noticed before today in her husband's eyes. Remorse and shame. (*It's a pity)* She thought. *Those regrets had come a little too late*. The heartache and pain he had inflicted on her over the years they had been married had ignited a burning flame that had numbed her. At this point, Caroline realized she needed to escape this God-forsaken marriage that had brought only misery to her life.

"Goodbye, John." A solitary tear wields down Caroline's cheek, making her turn away. "After tonight, we have nothing to say to each other." She headed for the door.

"Caroline, please." John pleaded. "Don't do this. I beg of you, don't turn your back on me; don't turn your back on us."

"I didn't, John. You managed *that* all by yourself." She inhaled deeply. (*Come on, Caroline. This has to be one of the best shows you'll ever have to put on. There's a room full of people on the other side of this door, just waiting to see you fail. Make sure and disappoint them.)*

Reaching for the doorknob, Caroline took two deep breaths before opening the door. Her eyes peered around to a room full of people. Who all seemed to have stopped what they were doing and shamelessly focused their attention in her direction. (*Come on, Caroline. You can do this. You have to.)* Once again, she cheered herself on.

"Caroline?" John's voice faded out by the music and the distance as she walked away.

"Goodbye, John." Caroline wiped her sweaty palms on her dress; lifting her shoulders, she held her head high and casually strolled to the bar.

"Figured you'd want a straight one." The barman placed a glass of scotch on the counter. "On the house." He gave her a reassuring wink with a crooked smile and patted her hand.

"Thanks, Jim." Caroline forced a smile before taking her drink. Lifting her glass, she turned around to face the roomful of noisy fans.

Who, for some reason or the other, found her life had brought them more excitement. Then, their stupid, dull existence.

"Cheers To the loser that just lost me. To the people in this room, I've managed to keep entertained, and to the lucky bastard I'll meet along the way on my life's journey." Her eyes roamed throughout the room before putting the glass to her mouth. She drained every last drop of her drink before placing the empty glass on the bar counter.

"Always going down with a bang, huh?" Jim laughed and shook his head as he watched Caroline elegantly stroll towards the exit and out of the nightclub.

John stood as he watched his wife walk out of his life for what could be the last time. Grabbing the glass from the table in a rage, he pelts it across the room, listening to the crushing sound of glass shattering into splinters, "Fuck!" he swears, pounding his fist into the wall.

"Come on, man." Jim reached over, bolting one of John's hands behind his back; he jerked him up against the wall.

"I've screwed up, man. I screwed up big." John vented through struggles

"Get a grip of yourself." Jim chucked at him again, placing his lower arms against his neck. "Yes! You screwed up, but from where I stand, you can do nothing about it now except pull yourself together and not draw unwanted attention. Got that!" Jim hunched at him again.

Feeling some pressure from John eased a bit when he nodded in agreement, Jim backed away slowly. "That's more like it." Looking down at John's bleeding knuckles. He tore a piece off his shirt, wrapping the cloth around John's hand. "There, that should stop the bleeding." Roughly, he pushed John's hand away.

"Let this night be a lesson for you. Go home, John!" Jim advised before he walked off, thinking how lucky John was that he went easy on him, for he had wanted to beat the living daylights out of this man for so long now. Once too many times, he had seen the blue, black marks on Caroline's body. Try as she may in cancelling them, her much too fair complexion would not permit it. If John liked maltreating his wife so much, maybe he should have tried it with someone his size (*like tonight was the perfect opportunity for him*). Jim thought.

CHAPTER FIVE

Carefully, he placed a single long-stem red rose and a handwritten note on the kitchen countertop before picking up the two bags he had packed. Throwing one across his shoulder while holding the other in his hand as he walked out of his house for what might very well be the last time.

Taking one last look around, John took a deep breath and reluctantly trudged towards the doorway, making sure to lock the door as he walked away. This house held so many precious memories, some good, some not so much, but all he treasured because they were with the one person who loved him the most.

It was a pity, for he knew deep within he never really loved Caroline. He had never returned her affection the way it should have been, as much as he hated admitting it. John realized he couldn't keep up with this pretence for much longer.

Young and naïve then, he thought he had found true love. However, not long after their marriage, John realized he had made a huge mistake by marrying Caroline. She was nowhere in his plans. She was torn at his side and kept him from enjoying the best years of his life.

Deep inside, John knew that this was one day coming. It was better now, tonight. Then, years down the road. This marriage wasn't doing either of them any good. It was slowly destroying them both. Caroline had become so dull, losing all her sparks in life. Nothing about her excited him anymore. He knew now that the things he had done over the past months were his way of telling her their marriage was over without saying the actual words to her. He knew a coward's way out, but it did work, and he had no regrets.

He threw his two bags into the trunk of the silver-grey Mazda. And he pulled his cell phone from his back pocket, dialing Logan's number.

"Hello." A rough voice at the other end echoed through the phone speaker.

"She's all yours, man. It's over between us." Even as the words left his mouth, John felt no remorse. If anything, he felt a deep sense of relief. Saying the words out loud had only made it official to him. John realized that he was finally free and loving this new feeling he was getting.

"What are you talking about, John?" Logan's voice once again echoed through the phone. "Where is Caroline?"

"Like I said, Logan. She walked out on me tonight and said something about fucking you." A long silence took over.

"Where is Caroline, John?" Logan's aggravation could be heard through the other end of the phone.

For some reason, John took great pleasure in this, wanting to taunt Logan a little more, considering that he would be blamed for all that had happened recently. "Can't you just shut up and listen for a bit? Is that too much to ask?" John slammed his fist into the car, creating a small dent in the hood. "Fuck!" He screamed in pain as blood sipped through the bandage around his hand again.

"Look, John, I am sorry for what has happened. But we should consider putting our differences aside for Caroline's sake." Logan said. His only concern was ensuring Caroline was safe. He didn't know why, but somehow, he felt responsible for what transpired tonight.

"I didn't call for your pity, Logan, neither do I want it." John's response was short and to the point. "And as much as I hate agreeing with you, my concern is the same as yours. Caroline's safety. After that, you can fuck your merry way for all I care." Flinching at the lancinating pain in his hand, John opened the car door and climbed inside, hoping that warming his hand up would help the pain. "Just let me know when she arrives, will you, Logan?"

"And what makes you think she'll come to me," Logan replied after a brief pause.

"I don't… I'm just going by what she told me?" John responded

"She's not coming here, John. I'm the last person. Caroline would turn to."

"Look, Logan. Seeing that it's over between Caroline and me. I think it's a good time for you to come clean." John reclined his seat, resting his head back. Making himself comfortable, he closed his eyes. "Fucking pain." He yelled out, hugging his arm towards him. "I mean, I'm no longer in the way. Am I? And considering that the only reason I got married to Caroline in the first place was to stop you from having her." his wicked laughter rang out to the opposite side of the phone.

"Naïve bastard!" Logan's fist clenched into a ball, grateful that John was not here in person, for there's no telling what he would have done to him. "Fuck you, John! You selfish, arrogant bastard!" Logan looked at the phone in his hand. "Fuck you for trying to turn this around on Caroline and me!"

"My, my… A whole lot of fucking going around here tonight." John laughed as he continued to provoke Logan.

"It just so happens that your wife is beautiful, John. Men will look, and men will lust. Which man wouldn't love making a woman like Caroline theirs? It's a pity you didn't realize what you had, John. The day will come, though, when you will and when you do. I promise you. It will be too late. You, sorry excuse for a piece of man!" Logan walked over to the small mini bar at his apartment, pouring himself a shot of whiskey.

"Is that a challenge, Logan? Are you implying that you can take my wife away from me?"

"Not implying, John. I am going to take Caroline away from you." Logan gulps down his whiskey, wiping his mouth with the back of his hand.

John lifted his head off the backrest of his car. "Care to put your money where your mouth is, Mr. Forrester, Sir." Smiling, he realized he had Logan exactly where he wanted him. He just never assumed it to be this easy.

"You know what, John? Just for fun, I might take you up on that wager." Logan poured himself another drink. "Name your price!" Logan quivered with rage. "That's considering you have anything left to lose." Logan decided to hit John below the belt, which would hurt him the most.

"Oh, I'm touched by your concern for me, Logan. But a gambler never thinks of losing. His number one rule. Always keep that in mind."

"Careful now, John. That's what got you into trouble in the first place." Logan cautioned.

Don't you worry about me, Logan? I have my way of putting things together. Let's say, Fifty thousand? Unless that's a little too steep for you." John mocked.

"That's what you call wager? Don't you think Caroline is worth a hundred times that?"

"I bet she is." (*To you, that is*) John smiled, resting his head again, this time feeling completely relaxed. (*Let the games begin*.) It would seem that Caroline is making me more money now than when we were together. A rush of excitement invaded his body. (*Why did I not think of this idea earlier*?).

CHAPTER SIX

"Caroline," Logan turned to see Caroline standing at the entrance of the doorway. A few strands of hair blew across her face caused by the door left open behind her.

"Why the surprised look, Logan?" Caroline kept her eyes glued to his as she strolled into the room. "I would think that you would be expecting me."

Logan watched as Caroline made herself comfortable sitting on the loveseat. She crossed one leg over the other, exposing quite a bit of her lovely, solid, well-structured legs.

"Well, are you going to offer me a drink, or are you just going to stand staring at my legs for the remainder of the night?" Her devious smile hinted at mischief.

"Oh yes, yes, I'm sorry. Where are my manners?" Logan turned towards the bar, placing his drink on the counter. "What would you like to have?" Casting a sideward glance in Caroline's direction, he grasped a bottle of 1992 Screaming Eagle Cabernet Sauvignon.

"I would normally say red wine, but this is a special occasion. So, I guess I'll have what you're having. Looks strong enough." Caroline felt an electrifying excitement inside when Logan's fingers slightly brushed against hers as she reached out to take the glass from his hand.

"I don't know where to start, Caroline. Except for..."

Caroline leaned forward, using her knees to support her elbows. "The clock is ticking, Logan. I believe the bet was for one night?" She looked up at Logan's old grandfather clock hanging to the left side of his minibar. Her attitude in speaking told him she was not interested in small talk or excuses.

Taking a sip of the red wine Logan had given to her. Caroline felt a little light-headed, for she had already indulged in a couple of beers before arriving at Logan's apartment. "Um, 1992 Screaming Eagle Cabernet Sauvignon." She slid the tip of her tongue across her lips and eyed him below her eyelids.

"I love it when a girl knows her wine."

"Oh, is that all you like?" she teased, her words holding double meaning.

"Among other things."

"Tic-toc, Logan." Caroline knocked the tip of her tongue to the roof of her mouth and eyed the clock behind his back.

It was to teach John a lesson, Caroline." Logan made himself comfortable sitting on a chair opposite Caroline. He folded his legs, taking a sip from his glass. Logan sat for a moment, unknowingly placing a finger under his chin while he studied Caroline for a bit longer.

"Damn, she is beautiful." Logan hoped his silent thought had not escaped his lips. Caroline had chosen to wear a red mini skirt with a white button-down tea shirt and black knee-high fuck me boots. Her hair was neatly wrapped in a bun with a few careless strands hanging loose. He noticed that now and again, she would try tucking them behind her ear. Oh, and that red blood stain lipstick. He couldn't tell what it was, but she used it exceptionally well—sending Logan's pulse racing with every movement of those luscious red lips. Logan could see Caroline standing there now with nothing but red lipstick, panties, and

boots. She would most certainly be an erotic sight—every man's fantasy.

"I want you to know, Darling. Nothing that happened in that nightclub tonight means you are obligated to me or have to do anything you don't want to."

"What if I want to?" Caroline glides her tongue slowly from one end of her lips to the next.

Her alluring action made Logan cough up. The last thing he expected was that kind of response from her. He awkwardly wiped the spilled drink on his shirt. "Well, it's like I told you, Doll." He glared at Caroline in a smug, complacent way. "It was only to teach John a lesson, nothing more. Besides, you should not have to pay the price for John and his ignorant arrogance."

"Hum..." Caroline took another sip, playfully spinning the wine around in her glass.

Logan couldn't help noticing Caroline's red mini skirt inching its way up her legs every time she moved. "Fuck." How he wanted to taste her, Logan could only imagine how heavenly it would be to suck the sweet juices from her pussy right at this moment, how just sliding his hand up her skirt and pulling her panties off would make him cum in his pants (*Come on Logan snap out of this. Down boy.)* his silent thought spoke to his cock. And he inadvertently stroked his cock.

Caroline's eyes pierced into Logan's, holding him captive when she parted her legs before him. She emptied the last of her wine, feeling the sweetness glide down her throat as she licked every last drop from her inviting lips. "Isn't that what you were wondering, Logan? Whether or not I had on panties," she said, the words almost as though she could read into his thoughts.

Logan knew he should be putting a stop to this while he still had some control left. But he was mesmerized. Lowering his eyes, Logan found himself spellbound by Caroline's seduction, needless to say, her naked pussy. "Oh fuck," The words involuntary escaped his lips.

"I figured they'd only get in the way, so why wear any?" Caroline eased her way over to Logan's chair, climbing him like a snake slithering up a tree. "Wouldn't you agree?" Whispering into his ear as she leaned over him.

Logan could feel the warmth of Caroline's breath and the gentle touch of her lips as they lightly brushed his earlobes. Shutting his eyes, he tried blocking out that the mountains of her two breasts were directly in front of his face and within mouth reach. "Ahem." Clearing his throat, he said, "I guess I would have to agree with you there." He gives her a crooked smile that curves the corner of his lips.

"I'd be crazy not to, right?" Logan took another sip of his whiskey. *Why couldn't he pull himself together*? He questioned himself. This was not the first time he'd found himself in a position like this, and he'd always managed to have some control. He was always able to walk away. So, then, what's so different about this? Once more, with the questions.

"Uh-huh." Caroline gently and slowly ran her fingers across his chest, biting at her bottom lips most enticingly.

"Okay, now that's enough. There's only so much a man could take."

He gently pushed her to the side. Jumping to his feet, Logan took Caroline's glass and walked over to the bar shakenly. (*Darn, his cock was ready to explode*.) Yes, he wanted Caroline. He had always wanted her, but not in this way, not when she felt obligated to give herself to him. He wanted her to want him the way he wanted her. Refilling their glasses, Logan returned to where he had left Caroline.

"I think we started this evening off on the wrong note, Caroline." Handing the glass to her.

Caroline put the glass to her nose, uninterested in what Logan said. "Don't you just love the aroma of red wine? Can't tell which is more addicting, the smell or the taste."

Logan watched Caroline gulp her drink down and then gently wipe the red stain off her lips with her index finger before placing the said finger into her mouth, sucking off every last drop of the red wine.

Darn... She was good. She knew what she was doing, and he must admit, she did it well. Caroline seemed to be a woman who knew what she wanted and processed the confidence to go after it. He admired that about her.

"Enough games." Caroline's mouth met with Logan's, slipping her tongue past his lips. Logan groaned eagerly, kissing back as the magic of Caroline's tongue explored his mouth. Not able to control this deep desire inside any longer, his hand slid around the small of her back, pulling her to him, wanting yet still more.

More of what she was offering. Logan listened to the popping of buttons falling to the ground one after the other as Caroline ripped his shirt off roughly, pushing him onto the sofa.

My, she was an aggressive one. He leaned backward, allowing her to have her way as his body danced to her rhythm. Falling to her knees, Caroline impatiently undid his pants, exposing the full hard length of his shaft as her hand circled and squeezed the total hardness of him. Her eyes met with his briefly. Her way of letting him know she was pleased with what she saw.

"Oh fuck, yes," Logan murmured as he felt the softness of Caroline's lips engulf the entire length of his cock into her mouth.

"Oh yes, baby." He reached forward, grabbing hold of her hair, watching as she expertly worked her mouth throughout every inch of his fully erected cock. Licking from the head down and back up again before placing it back into her mouth again and down her throat. "Oh, mercy." Logan reached for her. He needed to have her. He wanted to feel his cock inside her now.

"Down, boy," Caroline pushed him back to the sofa, gulping his whiskey. She spits most of it into his mouth before sucking it back out of his tongue. "You don't get to be in charge." She ordered him before making her way back to his cock.

Logan threw his head back and grabbed a handful of her hair, pushing her head down further as her lips descended over his cock once more. He was entirely and utterly beneath her spell, surrendering complete control to her.

Caroline listened to Logan's deep groan and the way he heaved his hips up to meet her as she deep, throat his cock into her mouth, sliding her lips around his cock. (It was time; he was ready.) She placed her mouth together with her hand around his shaft, covering the entire length as she continued to suck and squeeze simultaneously.

"Oh fuck, yes." Logan threw his head back, grasping her hair tightly, he pushed her head deeper.

Caroline could hear the groan deep within Logan's throat as the pulsing of his hard cock in her mouth released a white, salty substance. She looked up, meeting his eyes; she wiped her lips with her index finger and sucked the remainder of his liquid off before climbing to her feet.

"Leaving so soon?" Logan's guff voice intervenes as she makes attempts for the door. "You see Caroline, as much as I love having my cock sucked. I also love eating pussy." He slipped his hand around her waist with one jerk. He pulled her towards him.

"I need to leave Logan. John will be waiting."

"One night, sweetheart. Or have you forgotten?" She wasn't much of a liar. This much Logan could tell. Even if he had not gotten off the phone too long ago with John, he would have known by the way she lowered her eyelids, focusing her attention away from his piercing gaze.

"It's my turn to play, Darling." His tone was soft but, at the same time, demanding. Logan pinned her down on the sofa without allowing her time to react. A wicked smile curved at the corner of his lips. "You see, Caroline, two can play this game, and oh, how I love how you play." Logan slides his hand up her legs and beneath her skirt to her soft inner thighs.

"You're dripping, darling." He greedily licked at his lips before lowering his head between the soft silkiness of Caroline's legs.

Logan's witty voice annoyed Caroline some. He sounded too confident, yet Caroline still yielded to his every touch, even after knowing this. Gasping out in pleasure as Logan's tongue made its way into her, the involuntary movements of her hips raised to meet his mouth as her legs interlaced around his shoulders. Caroline's hand pushed at his head, wanting more of what he was doing, wanting to feel not only his tongue but his hard cock inside her.

"A real man doesn't need assistance to eat, my love." Logan pinned her hand to her side, restricting any more temptations she might have in assisting him. She was so wet right now that it wouldn't take much for her to erupt, but Logan wanted to play with this flaming ball of fire longer. Though he loved teasing her, he wanted her to know who was in charge.

"Not yet, my love, not until I tell you to." His tone was gentle. He wanted to enter her badly but decided to play the game her way. His tongue returned to her eagerly awaiting pussy, gently teasing her clit with his fingers.

"Now, Logan! Please now, she gyrated upwards, and screams of pleasure escaped her lips.

While sliding two of his fingers in and out of her. Logan's tongue made small circles around her pussy clit until Caroline's screams of pleasure filled the entire room.

CHAPTER SEVEN

"An ice-cold stag, please, Jim," Caroline ordered, climbing onto the barstool at the far end of the small lobby, wanting to drink the night away, hoping that somewhere along the line, she would forget the world, even if just for one night.

She had contemplated earlier on whether or not she should go to Maranda's but quickly decided against it, remembering that Logan would be there. The last thing she needed was another run-in with Logan, especially after what happened at his apartment last night, a night she would rather forget and not reminisce.

Caroline still hadn't figured out what had gotten over her last night, how she shamelessly and aggressively threw herself at Logan. What had she scared a bit, though, was realizing how Logan's audacious boldness excited her to the point where she surrendered herself fully, giving in to him and his daring erotic crimes. Last night, Logan had brought out a side to Caroline that she did not know existed. It was a side she would prefer to stay hidden, and she hoped that her secret would be safe with Logan.

Caroline figured her life was enough of a mess without adding any further complications to it. Plus, she was in no mood for Maranda and her matchmaking when it came to herself and Logan.

"On the house." Jim slides the beer down the smooth black granite countertop to Caroline, giving her a warm, welcoming smile. "It's always nice seeing you here. You look lovely as always, Caroline."

"Thanks, Jim," Caroline murmured, returning his warm smile. Remember how often she and Maranda would run away on weekends, mainly on a Friday night? They would come here and sometimes play pool. On other nights, they would dance the night away, neither having a care in the world. She took a sip of her beer, reminiscing. *"Those were the days."*

"They sure were, won't they?"

"Maranda," Recognizing the voice instantly without turning in the direction it was coming from. "What are you doing here?" Caroline took a long drink from her beer before placing the bottle on the counter. "How did you know where I would be?"

"Wasn't hard."

Caroline noticed from the corner of her eye how easy it was for her friend to sit on the high bar stool with little or no struggle. Maranda's height was one of the things Caroline had most admired about her friend.

"An ice-cold,"

"Stag." Jim finished Maranda's sentence, sliding the green beer bottle down the counter towards her.

Maranda laughed. "You haven't forgotten?"

"Forget my two favorite customers?" Jim smirked. "Never..." winking at both women.

"Oh, Jim. You always were a sweet talker." Maranda indulged the older man for a bit.

"Look, Maranda. I don't mean to sound ungrateful, but if you don't mind, I'd rather be alone tonight, please." Focusing her attention on her beer, she continued to spin the bottle around and around between the palms of her hands.

"Oh, I don't mind one bit." Maranda drank her beer. "Don't mind me, Hun. You go ahead and enjoy your alone time. I'm just here for the ambiance and the ice-cold beer." Maranda looked around, taking her bottle. She held it out. "Right, Jim." She took another gulp.

"Well, if that's what you want? You're in the correct place." Jim hustled over to the next side of the bar to fulfill another order.

"How did you find out?" Caroline broke the silence after a few minutes.

"Logan was worried about you."

"Logan told you?" Caroline's head shot up instantly, peering at Maranda suspiciously. She held her breath.

"Well, apparently, your husband was concerned about you, so he contacted Logan, then Logan also got worried, so he contacted me." Maranda rolled her eyes, finding humor in how she somehow caught herself in the middle of this charade.

"Oh, you mean that?" Finally, she could let the air out of her lungs once more.

"What did you think I mean?" Maranda squinted her eyes, closely observing Caroline.

You were utterly disregarding Maranda's question. Caroline let out a sarcastic laugh. "Worried about me?" She waved out to Jim, lifting two fingers. "Two cold ones." She shouted above the loud music. "A little too late for that, don't you think?"

"Well, Hun, you know what they say? You only miss the water when the river runs dry."

"Well," Caroline corrected.

"River, well." She waved her hand, realizing that Caroline was trying to hide something from her, but decided not to pursue the topic. "Who the fuck cares? You're finally rid of the son of a bitch." Holding out her beer to Caroline. "And that by itself is cause for celebration. Cheers, Hun. To new beginnings."

"Now that's something I can drink to." Listening to the knocking of glass as their bottle touched one another's.

"Cheers." Both ladies giggled

"I don't get it, though." Maranda gave Caroline a confused look. "One question still plagues me?"

"What's that?"

"Why, of all the people, why would John call Logan enquiring about you?"

"I think I might have had something to do with that." Caroline squinted her eyes, giving her friend a sly, cunning smile. She was quite pleased with herself for having accomplished what she had set out to do, and she was willing to make no apologies for any of it.

Jim interrupted, placing two beers on the counter. "Your secret admirer there." Tilting his head over to the pool tables section.

A tall, dark-skinned skin, well-built man dressed in faded blue jeans and a white buttoned-down shirt smiled and lifted his beer to the girls.

"You guys always did draw attention." Jim blurted out before returning to his job at hand.

"Suddenly, it just became scorching in here." Maranda spanned her chair back toward Caroline, pulling at her blouse. She blew down at her chest. "Mercy! Did you see the size of that hunk and those biceps? Oh, mercy, me." Taking a long, well-needed guzzle from her beer. "I need to cool off a bit." she fanned at herself with her fingers.

"I saw..." Caroline giggled at her friend. Maranda always had a thing for tall, handsome guys with broad chests, big shoulders, and eye candy. She would ever so often call them.

"Now, Caroline. There's nothing wrong with entertaining one's eyes, right?" lifting her beer to her mouth as her eyes once again carried across the room to the hunk standing at the pool table.

"Absolutely nothing... My friend, absolutely nothing indeed." Agreeing with Maranda one hundred percent on that remark. "Only I think this eye candy wants to entertain more than your eyes." Caroline burst out, chuckling.

"Ha, Ha, you think you're funny." Seeing no humor in her friend's outburst

"I do." Caroline continued laughing, teasing her friend

"Okay, enough with me and Mr. Hunk. What's his name there." Maranda tilted her head. "What's going on with you? Spill it!"

"Spill what?" Caroline asked with a confused expression. She shook her head. "I have no idea what you're talking about."

"Don't think I have forgotten. What did you tell the man that would make him believe you and Logan would spend the night in each other's arms?

"Oh, that." Caroline lifted her shoulders. "Not much, just that I was going to fuck the life out of Logan," she turned and ordered another round of beers.

"Oh, you bad thing... I will confess, I like your style." Maranda shook her head, quite proud of her friend. "Finally, you've started to grow a pair of balls. Good for you, darling." Knocking her bottle to Caroline's, "Cheers to that, Hun. One more thing to celebrate. And for the second time, you've made me proud of you."

"I'm proud of myself." Caroline blushed. "I think the beers have started getting to my head, Maranda." Caroline took another gulp and started to giggle.

"You think? Well, I know it's already gotten to mine." Both ladies giggled at nothing. Yet everything at this point seems to be funny to them.

For some reason, Caroline's eyes wielded tears amid her happiness as memories started resurfacing again. "What am I going to do, Maranda?" she bent forward, not wanting anyone to notice her tears.

"Do? I'll tell you what we'll do, sweetheart. We'll drink, we'll dance, we'll laugh, we'll let our hair down tonight." Maranda pulled the clip from her bun, shaking her hair loose. "Tonight, we forget everything and everyone. Tonight, we forget the world." Taking Caroline's hand. "Do we have a deal?"

"I guess." Wiping the tears from Caroline's cheek, giving her a gentle, caring smile. "That's not the reply I want, Caroline. I said do we have a deal?

"Yes, we have a deal," she said, looking at Maranda beneath her eyes childishly. "It was always hard saying no to you."

"That's a good thing, I think." Maranda held Caroline's hand and led her through the long corridor as they began their stumbling walk out of the elevator toward Caroline's room.

"Where is your key?" Maranda took Caroline's handbag from her. "Caroline, Honey, where are the keys to your room?"

Caroline placed her hand to her mouth, trying to stifle her giggles. "You're not going to find them in there." She watched as Maranda rampaged through her handbag for some reason, finding it hilarious.

"I'm not?" Maranda sigh. "Then why don't you tell me where I can find them."

Caroline placed her hand into the back pocket of her jeans and pulled a key out, dangling it in front of her friend. "Here it is." She is finding it difficult to keep her balance.

"Okay, now." Maranda rushed forward, holding out her hand to stop Caroline's fall. Placing Caroline's arms around her shoulders as she opened the door, stumbling a bit, she managed to guide Caroline towards the bedroom and safely onto the bed.

"You are such a good friend, Maranda. Have I ever mentioned it to you before?"

"I think you may have mentioned it a few thousand times tonight."

"Good, I'm glad." Caroline threw her arms around Maranda, rocking from side to side like a mother would her baby. "I love you, Maranda."

"And I love you." Maranda laughed, struggling to free herself from Caroline's embrace. "Now, let's say you lay back here and get yourself a good night's rest before you smother me to death." Pulling Caroline's shoes off, she pulled the blankets over her friend, tucking her in before wishing her a good night.

"Maranda," Caroline grabbed her friend's hand.

"Yes, Hun,"

"You're not leaving, are you?" Caroline's plea gave Maranda a sinking feeling in her gut.

"No, Hun. I'm not. I'll be right here when you awake in the morning." Maranda gave Caroline's hand a gentle pat. "It is going to be okay, Caroline. Now, get yourself some rest. We'll chat some more in the morning, okay?" Turning the lights off, Maranda turned around, taking one last look at Caroline, whose gentle snores told her she was already fast asleep.

"Well, look who decided to join the land of the living." Maranda poured a cup of coffee, handing it to Caroline.

"You're an angel, thanks." Caroline forced a smile, taking the cup from Maranda. She placed it to her lips with both hands, blowing gently before taking a small sip.

"Remind me again what a hangover feels like." She placed the cup on the small round coffee table and gently massaged it on her forehead.

"Exactly the way you're feeling right now." Maranda laughed, placing a plate with toast, bacon, and fluffy squabble eggs on the table. "You should eat something."

"You cooked?" Caroline stared at Maranda with a scared look on her face,

"Well, don't act so excited about it?" Maranda appeared slightly hurt for a moment but quickly brushed that feeling off. "Like that's ever going to happen, I ordered room service." Waving her hand, she dismissed Caroline's statement.

Unsurprised that Maranda could read her thoughts, Caroline took her coffee up again, cautiously taking another sip. "Was I much trouble last night?"

"Nothing I couldn't handle, baby girl." Maranda watched as Caroline greedily gobbled down every bit of food on the plate, helping herself to another portion of squabbled eggs and bacon. Judging from the way she ate, she wondered when the last time Caroline had herself a proper meal was.

It seems that Caroline had been depriving herself of the simple necessities of everyday living. Maranda's eyes also strayed down to the faded, washed-out blue jeans Caroline had worn once too often. But she concluded that Caroline had also been depriving herself of proper meals. She had lost so much weight. "What kind *of a man would do this to a woman*? Maranda silently asks herself.

"No pity, Maranda. Please," she said placing the fork back on her plate. "It's the one thing I don't think I'll be able to handle." Caroline's eyes were so full of tears that she unsuccessfully tried to blink away. "It's already an arduous situation as is." She quietly confessed through trembling lips.

"I'm sorry, Hun. It was never my intention." Grabbing the box of paper towels, Maranda strolled to the next side of the small breakfast table, wiping her friend's face. "You are so strong, Caroline. Much more, stronger than you give yourself credit for." Removing the tear-soaked hair off Caroline's face. "Look at me, Caroline. You don't need John in your life, Hun. You never did. Ask yourself one question?"

"What's that?" Caroline whispered through trembling lips. "What has the last five years brought to your life except for the misery and turmoil that John himself created? I might also be so bold to add." Maranda took Caroline's hand, almost dragging her off her chair and to the small bathroom mirror. "Look!" Pointing to the mirror, "It was always you, Caroline. You did it all by yourself. You made it this far, Hun. Surely you can go a little further." Maranda embraced her friend. "It's going to be okay, Caroline. You have to believe in yourself and your ability to do this."

Caroline blinked through her tears. Turning, she walked across the room onto the small balcony overlooking the small city area, already bustling with people and honking horns. Gripping at the railing, she looked down from the fifth floor of the sixty-foot drop to the ground pavement below. I can't say the thought had never crossed her mind a few times too many.

"It's not you, Caroline. You never were the giving up type." Maranda walked up to her.

Caroline's head lifted as she glanced at Maranda with red, teary eyes.

Maranda looked at her friend, confirming her suspicions. "You're a fighter, Caroline. You always have been. You are one of the strongest people I know. So, life throws you a few curve balls here and there." She folded her arms across her chest, letting out a sarcastic laugh. "A few too many, if you ask me, but I think you've always managed to overcome triumph. It was one of the many things I've always admired about you, Caroline. Your ability to pick yourself up and keep going."

"Wow! That was quite a powerful speech. You should be given a medal for making people feel good about themselves." Caroline gave her friend a slight smile. "I never knew you felt that way about me."

"Are you kidding me? You've been my hero for as long as I can remember. You're my role model, Caroline. I couldn't handle half the crap that you've been through." Maranda eagerly responded, "So when you think people aren't watching," she rubbed Caroline's upper arms. "Guess what, Hun, they are. You never know when your story might be someone else inspiration. Plus, many people are waiting to see you fail, Caroline. They stand on the sidelines like vultures, watching and waiting for that day. Prove those bitches wrong." She squeezed Caroline's hand. "You take every stone thrown your way and build yourself a darn castle. You do what you must, whatever it takes but prove the motherfuckers wrong." Her voice lowered. "But most of all, Caroline. Please, do it for you. Make yourself proud."

"Well, if I had no intentions before, I do now. Thank you so much, Maranda." Giving her friend a warm hug. "What did I to deserve you in my life? I don't know, but I am glad you are part of it." I am not waiting for a response. "I think your pep talk was exactly what I needed to remind me of who I am. I'd be lying if I told you I didn't know this was coming. I've known it for a while now." She rested her elbows on the balcony and leaned back. "And I guess, if I were to be completely honest with myself, I've already accepted and come to terms with it. Possibly even before I walked out on John and our marriage, it had been a thought that had plagued me for months now. I guess I just wanted to be sure that when I did decide to leave, I'd have no regrets."

"Then what is the problem?" Maranda shook her head. "If what you say is, in fact, the truth, I would think you would have already gotten over the worst part of it... No?"

Caroline cast a sideward glance in Maranda's direction. "One would think so, wouldn't they? Only that isn't the worst part. Not at this given moment anyway."

"Huh, then what is? I don't understand?"

Playfully biting at her bottom lip, Caroline felt the weight of the entire world had dropped on her shoulders. "The bank is literally down my throat about the mortgage payments. I face being evicted in just a matter of weeks. The car payments still have not been paid." Her hand lifted and then dropped to her side. "I'm surprised they haven't started repossessing yet." The sheer futility of her situation had started to exasperate her. "Oh..." laughing out, more to herself. "And did I neglect to mention I got retrenched?"

"You got what? When did this happen?" Maranda's eyes widen

"Yep..." Caroline nodded. "Two days ago, I lost both my marriage and job in a matter of just two days. I think I broke a record with this one, huh? It's like the universe is trying to tell me something." Dropping her shoulders, she sighs. "What am I to do, Maranda, and how do I do this myself?"

"Okay... I understand what you're saying, but I don't think you're looking at this logically, Hun."

"What does that mean?"

"In case you haven't noticed, Caroline. You have been doing this by yourself." Maranda pulled up a chair, sat down with legs wide apart, and leaned forward. "You were the one that kept things together,

Caroline. You were the one that kept things going. Don't you see, John was the one that needed you. You didn't need him, Hun? You never did."

"Son of a bitch gambled everything away, Maranda. She could no longer hold back everything!" the contempt in her voice. "I had no idea it had gotten this bad until a few weeks ago. I'm left with nothing except his twenty-eight dollars in my account. There's no food in the house. I'm out of a job."

She buried her chin into the palms of her hands. "When did I get here, Maranda? How could I have allowed things to reach this bad?" her questions were intended more for herself than her present company. "And do you know what the irony of the situation is?"

"What's that?" Maranda asked, biting back the tears that stung her eyes.

"I have no clue where to start from. Tell me," she asked. "Who does one turn to when there's no one left? And what does one do when backed against a wall."

"You do what you have to, Caroline. Whatever it takes. Here, come with me." Maranda got to her feet and headed for the door.

"Where are we going?" Caroline snatched her handbag, almost running to keep up with Maranda.

"Do you trust me?" Maranda's words echoed while running down the steps through the corridor and out of the hotel, with Caroline tailing close behind.

"I'm almost afraid to answer." Caroline climbed into the passenger side of the car, buckling her seatbelt.

"Haven't I always wanted the best for you?"

"I guess..."

"Then, believe me when I tell you everything will be okay." She cast an at the review mirror before pulling onto the road.

"Well, I guess it can't get any worse, can it?"

"Now that's the mindset you need." Maranda patted Caroline on the leg, winking at her. The remainder of their journey was driven in complete silence. And Caroline placed her head halfway through the window, welcoming the windy breeze blowing her hair violently through the air.

CHAPTER EIGHT

Maranda pulled her car into the Central Plaza Mall, which was centered outside the small country town about an hour and a half drive from where the girls lived. She pulled the car into the first available parking area she saw vacant. "Wait here for a few minutes, will you." unbuckling her seatbelt.

Caroline nodded, laying her head back.

"I'll be back in a few." She utters, walking a short distance off.

Caroline sat back and watched her friend's face light up as she climbed into a grey 4by4 that pulled up beside her. Smiling, she exited mere minutes later and blew a kiss the driver's way.

"Hiding things, are we?" Caroline mocked as Maranda approached

"It's not what you think, Caroline." Maranda rolled her eyes. "Remember when I asked if you trusted me?"

"Oh, good lord! What have you done, now?" Giving Maranda a Suspicious glare.

"Just trust me on this, will you? Come on." She waved

Caroline watched Maranda approach the silver van, now parked next to a stone wall at the far end of the mall parking lot.

"Are you coming or not." Maranda turned, taking two steps backward, her voice carried through the wind to Caroline.

Caroline inhaled deeply. Reluctantly, she strolled towards Maranda.

"I know you'll probably want to kill me for this right now, but you must realize you are in a tight situation. You see, Caroline, sometimes we are all pushed into situations where we have no choice but the one presented before our eyes, if you get my drift."

"Okay," Squinting her eyes. "You sound as though you're going to pimp me out." Caroline jokingly laughed.

"Logan is here, Caroline."

"What!" She frowned, quickly turning her head in the direction of the van. "Here, now?"

"Yes, here, now. And he wants to meet with you."

"Maranda," Caroline dragged the name with condemnation.

"I'll be in the mall," Maranda revealed. "Don't call me." She pushed her tongue out at Caroline in a childlike manner.

"What, no!" Caroline watched as Maranda threw her handbag over her shoulder and proceeded towards the mall entrance, paying no natural mind to her ranting. "You can't do this to me. Maranda." Her voice faded, realizing that she already did.

The passenger side of the van door opened before her. Caroline watched as Logan pulled his hand back inside the van. She stood gazing at the open van door, clearly indicating what he expected of her.

Her legs suddenly went numb. Try as she may, they refused to move. (*Come now, Caroline. You can do this.)* She cheered herself on. (*All you have to do is place one foot in front of the other*) she nervously trudges closer to the open van door. Memories of their last night's encounter replayed vividly in her mind.

Logan's smirk annoyed her some. His arrogant attitude was way bigger than his cock if one were to ask her.

Caroline wiped the sweat from her forehead with the palms of her hands as she entered the vehicle, appreciating the van's relaxed air condition. "The heat out there is outrageous today. "Thanks." Gingerly patting at the drips of sweat that leaked down her neck and between the mountains of her breast.

"Nice cleavage." Holding no shame in staring down at Caroline's breast and the way her hands moved gracefully over her hot body as she tried to cool herself down.

"Haven't your mother ever taught you that staring is rude?" She frowned at him

"She did... But my father, on the other hand, taught me never to let a great opportunity pass me by." Logan replied with yet another smirk.

"What do you want from me, Logan?" her question was blunt and concise. She was leaving no room for misconception.

"Well, my lovely bunny, I would have thought you'd figure that out by now. I want you, Caroline. I apologize if I left any doubt in your mind about that." He said with an intense gaze.

"Wow, I can't believe you said that out loud." Biting her bottom lip, unable to break free from the intensity in his eyes.

"Let's just say I'm a man who knows what I want. And what I want, I pursue."

"And do you always get what you want?" The words escaped her mouth daringly.

"Always," He assured, with certainty.

Caroline turned away, breaking eye contact, and she exhaled slowly. He had won this round. Logan's bold demeanor unnerved her, and she shifted uneasily in her seat. But she had no intentions of letting this man get the better of her. "In that case, I wish you luck in your future endeavors."

"I'm glad you feel that way." Logan switched the vehicle off, exiting the van. He casually walked over to Caroline's side, opening the door for her. "Let's take a walk in the mall."

Caroline gave no resistance when Logan reached out, taking her by the waist. She placed both hands on his broad shoulders when he lifted her down. Even in her blue five-inch heels, Logan's height overpowered hers, making her feel a little intimidated.

"Coffee?" Logan broke the silence as they strolled through the colorful hallway of the vast mall. He grabbed hold of Caroline's elbow, tugging her towards the cafe. "I think it's mocha, right?" he joined the line leading up to the cashier.

"Fresh brew with a little milk. Hold on to the cinnamon and sugar." She answered before she jerked her arm from his grip. Viewing around, Caroline walked over to one of the vacant tables where she sat in awe, taking in the sight of this magnificent beast. With feet spread apart and arms folded across his chest. Logan had the look of a bodyguard. For some reason, she found humor in that thought. Imagine having your very own bodyguard. A small smile curved her lips at the idea.

Logan was indeed the gentle but rigid kind of a man. He had always kept himself clean-shaven. He was a tall, dark, good-looking man with broad shoulders and a chest that always seemed to push at his buttons, making his shirt appear a lot tighter than it was. Yes, he was a pleasant sight for any woman's eyes—looking at the two red-heads on the table next to her laughing and enjoying their view of the eye candy that stood at the counter. Caroline could only imagine what their conversation about Logan could be.

"Calm down, girls." Caroline rocked her chair slightly back. "He already got himself a husband." A mischievous smile curved her lips when she noticed how quickly both women's facial expressions changed to grim, as a pose to the amusement it held before their recently disappointing news.

Caroline quickly lowered her lashes and peered away when Logan glanced in her direction. What is it about this man that intimidated her so, intimidation mixed with a bit of excitement? She wasn't sure how well they combined, but deep inside, she knew the excitement thrilled her.

Her eyes followed Logan's every move when he took the two cups of coffee from the cashier and walked over to the small counter at the side of the café, pouring milk into one of the cups. Her thoughts simultaneously took her back to the last night they spent together and how their bodies danced to the beat of each other tune.

Even now, she could feel Logan's hands caressing between her legs. She squeezed them together and tried to focus on the man walking towards her table. His broad frame drew closer with three strides from his long legs.

"Here you go." Logan passed one of the cups to Caroline.

"Thanks." Lifting the lid off her cup, Caroline blew at the steam before sipping.

"Are you scared of me, Caroline?" Logan sat down, his eyes following her every movement.

"Not in the least bit." She took another sip from her cup and focused on the café entrance, trying to bring her mind off his suggestive, erotic ogle.

"Do I make you nervous?" his eyes burnt with intensity

"No," she whispered with a trace of uncertainty. She needed to find a way to lead this conversation away from her. Logan was getting a little too close for comfort. "Aren't you going to drink your coffee before it gets cold?" she asked.

"I would," he paused, spinning the cup. "But I prefer my coffee black."

"I don't understand?" Caroline followed Logan's eyes to the coffee she was holding. "Oh, I'm so sorry." She awkwardly exchanged cups. "I didn't realize." Her cheeks turned to a flushed pink.

Logan couldn't help the smirk on his face. "So, I don't make you nervous, huh." He teased, taking a sip from his coffee.

"I'm still looking for your humor, 'cause in case you haven't noticed? You're the only one laughing." She stated, clearly not enjoying his sarcasm and being made fun of.

"Cheer up, Bunny. I wasn't laughing at you; I was laughing with you." he reached out, pinching her nose playfully.

Slapping his hand away, "What do you want, Logan?" she clenched her teeth.

"Gay, my ass!" the two redheads passed by, sneering Caroline's way.

"What are they on about? Who's gay?" Logan asked.

"You." Caroline lifted her coffee to her mouth with a puckish look.

Confused about what she was speaking about, Logan decided it best to refrain from pursuing. "Maranda told me about your predicament, Caroline."

"She shouldn't have done that." Cutting him across sharply.

"Maybe so," Logan reached out, taking her hand. "But she did, and I can't turn a blind eye." He pulled an envelope from his jacket, sliding it across the table to Caroline. "I want you to have this, and please don't refuse."

"What is it?" Caroline peered inside the envelope. "I can't take this." She stared at Logan wide-eyed, pushing an undisclosed sum of cash back to Logan, shaking her head. "There is no way I can accept this. It just wouldn't feel right."

"Please, Caroline, I want you to." his hand covered hers. "Consider it a loan if necessary, but please don't refuse me." Logan pleaded, holding her gaze

Feeling self-conscious, Caroline stood up and folded the envelope before pushing it into the back pocket of her jeans. "I can't promise you that will be anytime soon, Logan, but I will pay you back."

"I'm sure." He shook his head. He wanted to tell her there was no need for her to do anything of the sort, but he knew she would disagree. "I would like you to know something about me, Caroline."

"Why?"

"Why? Because I want our relationship to be based on honesty."

"Our relationship?" Caroline looked at him, surprised at his choice of words

"Yes, Caroline, our relationship."

Caroline laughed. "I'm sorry to burst your little bubble, Logan." she leaned forward across the table. "I'll let you in on a little secret. We don't have a relationship," she whispered, winking at him with a light touch of sarcasm.

Logan reclined himself on the chair, tapping his fingers on the table. "Not yet."

"Not ever." Holding the same sarcastic tone, Caroline stared at him without blinking

"Time will only prove you wrong." He teased.

"What was it you so eagerly wanted me to know about you, Logan?" fed up with his childish games.

"I'm married."

Caroline almost choked on her coffee when it drooled out of her mouth across the table. "Did I just hear you correctly?"

"You did." Logan nodded but offered no further explanation.

Turning away, Caroline burst out with laughter. "Then what do," she held back, staring at Logan in amazement. "If I may be so bold to assume?" Caroline waited for his permission to continue.

Logan held his hand out to her. "By all means, please do." Propping a finger beneath his chin, he focuses his full attention on Caroline.

"Let me guess," she said. Leaning back, she folded her arms, looking at Logan through squinted eyes. "Stuck in a marriage with lack of communication, no love, no passion, and most importantly for a man, that is, no sex stuck in the same old routine day after day, night after night. Nothing new to look forward to? Must get pretty boring, huh?"

"I must admit it does," Logan answered.

"I would ask why stay, but I think I already know the answer to that question." she tapped her long pink polished nail on her lips. "Why would any man decide to stay stuck in a loveless marriage, kids?" observing his reaction, she placed both elbows on the table and leaned forward. "How many?"

It amazed Logan how accurate and précised Caroline was in every bit of information she offered. "Two girls." His eyes dropped briefly.

"A man like you needs to be fed, Logan." She lifted her eyebrows, "Am I not right? Men like you need a little excitement or, in your case, a lot. It's like playing a good game of poker. The higher the stakes, the more thrill you get out of it, and you need that thrill. It's like adding fuel to your van. Without it, you might as well be dead." Caroline slid her feet up Logan's leg, making sure she kept study eye contact.

Logan whimpered and gave her a sly grin. Nothing Caroline did lacked excitement, which had him both mesmerized and spellbound. She always left him craving for more.

"Tell me something, Logan." Caroline slides the tip of her tongue across her lips. "What do you hope to gain by sharing this bit of information?" licking her lips again. "What do you expect from me?" Watching him squirm in his chair as her toes made small gentle strokes up and down his now fully erected cock.

"Well, my lovely Bunny." He replied, "As you said in so many words, I'm hoping you would fill that space by making me feel alive again." His hand reached beneath the table, making a slight adjustment to his cock as he shifted uneasily in his seat.

"Hum. Why me?" she asked confidently.

"Because, Caroline. You excite me."

She lifted her brows as if to point out the obvious. "You are married? Yes?"

"Forgive me if I'm wrong here, but you seemed briefly excited about that fact a short while ago."

"What exactly are you proposing, Logan? Forgive me if I'm wrong here, but this is a proposal. And if so? What's in it for me?"

"Uh, um." Logan placed his elbows on the table and incline forward. "Maybe I'm reading you all wrong, but you and I are the same, Caroline, whether you choose to acknowledge this fact or not."

"I'd like to know how you came to that conclusion." Her eyes narrowed slightly

"You like excitement, sweetheart. You live for it. John could never fuck you the way I can." Logan smirked

"And you think you can fuck and excite me?"

He shook his head. “Nope, not think, I know. Your fingers, for instance,” his eyes dropped to her hand. “Look at the way it circles the rim of your cup.”

“That proves nothing.” Her eyes involuntary dropped to her fingers.

“The way your lips quiver whenever I’m close.” Logan continued in a low, seductive tone. His eyes dropped to her lips. “Even now, I can tell you’re still thinking about the last night we shared and how I made you feel.” He reclined and placed a finger to his lips. “I bet you’re anxious and eager for the next time. Aren’t you?”

“In your dreams, only.” Caroline shot back. “Apparently, you can’t seem to get it out of your mind either or you wouldn’t have brought it up.” She watched Logan walk around the booth, inching himself next to her.

“Either, does that mean I was right?” he pushed a strand of her hair behind her ear, gazing into deep brown eyes. “I bet you’re wet.” He whispered, brushing his lips slightly against her earlobes, barely allowing her time to react. Logan’s hand reached beneath the table.

Caroline’s eyes widened and swiftly lifted to meet with Logan’s.

“Shhh.” Logan's finger went to his lips. “Drink your coffee, sweetheart.” He tugged her soft lace panties to the side and slid a finger into her soft, wet flesh. He guided his free hand behind her back and detained her to his side.

Caroline gasps out, closing her eyes. She tried to shut out the rest of the café. It was useless trying to stop Logan, this much she knew. Besides, once again, her body betrayed her for the second time in two days, granting Logan the right to do with it as he pleases. She was so hot for him right now that there was nothing she could do to stop his forbidden seduction.

“No, Caroline, you don’t get to do that,” Logan whispered in a husky voice. “Open your eyes, darling.” The hot air from his mouth brushed past her cheek, making her squirm that much closer to him. “Look at me,” he ordered. “I want to see the look in those eyes when you’re overflowing with ecstasy.

Besides, I don't think it wise to draw attention to ourselves." A mischievous grin curved the corners of his lips. As he pondered on circling the tip of her clit with his thumb while allowing a finger to slide into her, a soft moan escaped Caroline's lips. And Logan took glee when he felt a stream of hot fluid and the stiffening of her body against him.

"That's my girl," he pulled his hand out from beneath the table. "You're mine, Caroline. The sooner you learn that the better off you'll be."

"You're an ass, Logan." Caroline pushed her chair back and got to her feet. "Are you going to take me home, or do I walk?"

"It's going to be a long walk." Squinting, his eyes held a glow of mischief. "Where are you going? I'm not finished with you?"

"I'm done with you."

Logan could hear the annoyance in her voice. "In that case, you leave me with no choice?" he stood up. "After you, my Bunny."

"Smartass." She murmured and stormed past him.

"Wait up, Caroline." Even with his long strides, he almost ran to catch up with her. "What's the rush?" He grabbed hold of her elbow. "Slow down, will you."

"I'm in no mood for your games, Logan." Jerking her arms from him, she glared at him.

"Fifteen minutes, it's all I'm asking."

Caroline let out a deep breath. "Fine, fifteen minutes. After that, you take me home. No excuses."

"No excuses, I promise." Holding his hand out front

"Where are you taking me?" Caroline walked alongside Logan, noticing how he made his steps shorter to accommodate her slow pace.

"Here we are." Her bewildered expression gave him a sense of satisfaction.

Caroline slowly looked around. "What is this? I don't understand?" Lifting her brows, she turned to him.

"Choose whatever you like, sweetheart."

"Wow, you're kidding me, right?"

"Why would I do that?" Assuring her that he meant every word

Caroline walked over to the glass cases. Everything in the store was shiny and glittery: Diamonds, pearls, silver, gold, every woman's dream.

"Can I help you, Mam? Is there anything special you would like to get today?" the pleasant young woman politely offered assistance.

"Every woman's dream indeed, but not mine." She looked at the young lady, "No, I'm sorry, dear, not today." Caroline watched the color drain from the woman's face, obviously disappointed she could not make the sale.

Caroline sneaked a peek at Logan. Once again, he stood at the doorway with his hands folded across his chest and parted legs as usual. *(Gosh, darn it, there it was again; just the mere sight of him drove her body insane.)*

Logan strolled towards her with his hands entwined behind his back. "Do you see anything you like?"

"No." Keeping her response short

"Come on, Caroline, something must catch your eyes."

"Take me home, Logan. That was the deal." She saunters towards the store exit, not waiting to see whether he was behind.

CHAPTER NINE

Logan poured a glass of whiskey, gaggling the drink in his mouth before swallowing. Refilling his glass again, he pulled a pack of cigarettes out of his pocket, knocking the box against his hand before using his teeth to pull one out. "Where the fuck is my lighter?" his hand patted at his jacket. "Darn it." he only now remembered he had loaned his lighter to a homeless man on his way home, never bothering to take it back. Rampaging through the counter draws he found a used lighter and breathed a sigh of relief.

Grasping his glass, Logan walked towards the back door and into the garden's ground. Taking a long drag from his cigar, he lifted his head and slowly exhaled, watching the smoke part ways as it lingered into the night's air. It was a bad habit he needed to quit, and he scolded himself countless times. But not today. He was sure of that.

Being away from home, Emma and the girls were a type of freedom he could not explain. Emma and Logan had been married for the past ten years, not that it was a bad marriage. It just became routine. Their marriage had lost all sparks. More so in the bedroom where sometimes even weeks would pass without sex. Lovemaking was entirely out of the question until Logan, tired of trying, finally gave up and fell into the same old dull, monotonous routine himself.

He often finds himself by the desk in his home office at night, watching porn and pleasuring himself after coming home from a hard day's work, only to find Emma asleep and a note on the kitchen table saying dinner was in the oven.

His marriage was in shambles. It had lost all excitement. Intimacy was something a man desperately needed. A man needed his ego stroked. He needed to be loved and cared for, bottom line a man needed his wife to fuck the life out of him after a hard day's work at the office, none of which he was awarded, and also the reason why guilt was the furthest thing on his mind at this given time.

So now that the excitement was slowly returning in his life, he'd be darn if he allowed the opportunity to pass him by. Putting his cigar out, Logan gulped the last whiskey down as memories of the previous few weeks kept replaying. He half expected Caroline to get back to him about his proposal by now, but as it turns out, she needed more convincing. Logan bent his head, smiling to himself. "Nothing like a good chase makes the game that more exciting."

Logan looked at the time on the gold band wristwatch he opted to wear that day. He would have to get back indoors and grab a quick shower if he was to keep his dinner plans with Mr. Henderson, one of the company's most significant shareholders.

Mr. Henderson was in town for a few days but had pleaded with Logan not to inform anyone about his presence. Wanting some time off and away from the stress of work, among other things, he invited a few of the guys over for dinner, drinks, and a night of poker.

Logan walked up the steps and adjusted his tie before reaching out to ring the doorbell to the old enormous mansion.

"That's what I've always liked about you, Logan," Mr. Henderson opened the door and reached out his hand to Logan. "Count on you to always be on time." Mr. Henderson's loud laughter echoed throughout the large hallway. "Come in, come in." Stepping aside to grant Logan entrance into the room. "I don't know about you, Logan, but I'm excited about starting this night."

"Drinks, Sir." The butler walked over to Mr. Henderson with a tray of beers in hand.

"One for me and one for you." Handing the green bottle of beer to Logan. "Cheers, my friend." he lifted his bottle to Logan's.

"Cheers, Sir." Knocking his bottle against Mr. Henderson's, Logan put the beer to his mouth, "Ahh..." Holding the beer out, he looked at the bottle in his hand, "Stag has always been a man's beer and a darn good one at that, too."

"Oh yes, I quite agree." Laughter filled the room. "Get the door for me, will you, Logan." Mr. Henderson threw over his shoulders as he scampered out of the room.

"Well, this is a surprise. I wasn't aware that you got demoted to a butler now." holding on to Clair's hand, he brushed past Logan.

"John," Logan greeted, closing the door behind them

"I hope it pays well enough."

"I see you wasted no time in getting yourself a replacement." Logan folded his arms, untouched by John's touches of sarcasm.

"Oh, you mean her. This is...."

"I know who she is, John. Everyone in town knows who she is."

"My misunderstanding. I thought you wanted to fuck her as well. No pun intended, but I observed how you eagerly awaited the side-line like the dog you are for my remnants the first time!" His eyes pierced into Logan's

It took Logan two long strides to close the gap between himself and John. "Why you little scumbag!" grabbing John by his shirt collar Logan chucked him up the closest available wall.

"What's the matter, Logan," he wrestled to get loose. "Which part didn't you like, the part where I called you a side-line dog?" He continued his taunting, "I bet it's the part where I called my wife leftover scrapes?" his laughter was filled with contempt.

"Come on, guys," Mr. Henderson's voice traveled across the hallway. "Let's play nice." Nearing the distance between himself, Logan, and John.

"Count your lucky stars. Mr. Henderson showed up when he did," Logan told John in a hushed tone.

Clair rushed to John's side, helping him off the floor. "Get! Your hands off me!" tugging his elbow away from her, adjusting his shirt collar back into place, he stared at Logan, staggering to regain his balance. "Tell me, Logan, where is the little slut? I would have thought she would be here with you tonight."

"Dinner is being served." Mr. Henderson announced, "Come on, folks, this way. There would be plenty of times for your little lovers to quarrel later. "And who is our unexpected guest?" taking Clair's hand, he brushed his lips slightly over her palm. "It's a pleasure to meet you, my dear. It's a pity my young gentlemen friends here don't know how to conduct themselves in the presence of a lady." He smiled, taking her hand as he led the way to the dining room. "Forgave them. They are young yet, got much to learn." He patted her hand before pulling a chair out for her to sit.

John cast an eye around the table before leaning sideways. "So, have you fucked her yet?" he placed the bowl of mashed potatoes back on the table.

Logan could feel the pounding of his heartbeat and the quickening of his pulse as John continued to deploy his insults.

"I'm only asking because I have a stake in this too, you know, bitch goanna be horny as hell hasn't been laid in months. I should know I fucked her last."

Logan took a deep breath and jumped to his feet, grabbing John's neck.

"Enough!" Mr. Henderson shouted, slamming his hands on the table. "I've had quite enough out of the both of you."

"Hell! You're not worth it." the tightening of Logan's jaw and his blood-shut eyes told a story as he shoved John, watching him and the dinner chair tumble over to the ground.

"I'm truly sorry things had to turn out this way tonight, Mr. Henderson." Fixing his tie, Logan humbly apologized, "But I think it's best if I take my leave now. Don't bother getting up; I can see myself out." Logan glared at John before walking away.

CHAPTER TEN

"Oh, hi, Caroline. It's been a while since we've seen you." Natalie eagerly jumped to her feet, giving Caroline a bright, cheerful smile as she entered the café. "Will you be having your usual cappuccino today?" Natalie grabbed a paper cup and started preparing the coffee before hearing Caroline's response. Caroline had been a customer of theirs from the first day the coffee shop opened.

"Yes, please," Caroline placed her handbag on the table before she slumped into her favorite chair. Tipping her head backward, she closed her eyes briefly, taking several deep breaths. She had been job hunting all day with no luck, and now the day's tiredness was starting to catch up with her.

"Here you go." Natalie placed the cup on the table. "Would there be anything else?"

"Nope, that will be all, Nat, thanks." Offering the girl, a friendly smile.

Caroline often hid away at the well-tucked little cozy coffee shop called Nasa Café. The small business was always well-kept and was managed by two pretty-looking sisters. Their customers were always greeted with bright, friendly smiles, which matched perfectly with their social services. The well, hidden Café was nestled away at a little corner outside town, about a forty-five-minute drive from the countryside. It was hardly ever visited by any of Caroline's villages, which was one of the things Caroline liked most about it.

Aside from the heavenly aroma of freshly brewed coffee. The donuts, cupcakes, and homemade ice cream were simply mouth-watering. Nasa Café was like Caroline's private little gateway, a place she could come to whenever she wanted to be invisible to the rest of the world.

She cast her eyes over to the clock on the side wall at the café, grabbed her handbag and coffee, and threw some money on the table before rushing out the door.

Caroline pulled her car into the driveway of her house and picked her cell phone up.

"Hello." Maranda's voice echoed from the other end of the speaker.

"Hi, Maranda. I think I might be coming down with something.

"And what might that be, the case of lying?" Maranda's voice resonated through the phone.

"See now, you're being a bitch again, a mean one at that too."

"Tell me something I don't already know, Darling." Taking no offense to Caroline's derisive remark.

"I'm sorry to have to cancel on you at the last minute like this, but I've been on my feet since the break of dawn, and I'm way too exhausted even to consider going anywhere tonight, let alone having fun. Could you be a dear and give my apologies to Logan, please."

"I will, but he's not going like it."

"He'll survive."

"I'm sure. You get some rest. I'll buzz you in the morning."

"Yep, will do. Thanks for understanding, Maranda. You're the best." Caroline cut off, happy to get out of tonight's commitment with Logan and Maranda.

God, how handy a bottle of wine would have come in on a night like this, recapping how she had poured every drop of alcohol down the sink. She was still scolding herself for that one stupid act.

She reached for a towel and wrapped it around her naked body, stepping out of the shower. Sliding her hand on the railing, she walked down the stairs and into the kitchen, thanking God that she'd at least had the half sandwich left over from breakfast this morning.

Used to her now empty refrigerator, Caroline had programmed herself to skip meals whenever necessary. She had grown used to sleeping with an empty tummy recently. But tonight, her stomach was rumbling so badly that she needed to get something down.

She would either have to find a job soon or risk being obligated to Logan. By dipping into the cash he loaned her, that was a thought she did not want to entertain. A strong wind gust indoors. And she quickly rushed over to the front door and pushed it shut. "Darn it!" How could I be so careless?" Scolding herself, "I could have sworn I'd locked that door." She mumbled with a wave of dismissal.

"You did." Came the familiar voice from the kitchen doorway.

"Logan!" Caroline's hands instantly raised to her chest. "You startled me."

Logan held a bottle of red wine in his hand. "Maranda said you couldn't make it to the dinner, so I figured it best to bring it to you." he took a few steps forward. "Pizza?" he asked, signaling towards the kitchen.

"Are you crazy, Logan?" she snapped, glaring at him wide-eyed. "You can't just walk into people's houses uninvited."

"I didn't, Bunny." He placed the open bottle of wine on the counter. "Glasses, please?"

Caroline signaled to the cupboard door over his head. "How did you get in here, Logan?" She stood with her arms folded across her chest and frowned at him.

"Nice outfit." Logan's eyes widen slightly, smirking. He peered at her from the head down before handing her a glass of red wine. "Now, to answer your question, I was going to knock first, but," he pushed his hand into the front pocket of his jeans, pulling several keys out. "I figured you left them in the lock for me." Dangling the bunch in front of her

She uncrossed her arms and stared at him, drawing herself up to full height. "Oh, bloody hell." She dropped her shoulders and grabbed the keys from his hand. "I need to stop doing that; she reached for the glass of wine and gulped it all in one drink.

"You're quite thirsty." Logan looked at her, impressed; he refilled her glass.

"Also staved." She walked over to the cupboard, grabbing some napkins and two plates while Logan opened the box.

"So, you're not angry at me anymore?"

"I'm always angry at you." She replied in an easy-going manner before biting into a slice of pizza.

"I wonder why that is?" He tilted his head back with a smug grin that curved the corner of his lips.

"Certainly not what in your perverted mind." She fixed him with an unwavering stare.

"More wine?" he reached for the bottle, "So, tell me, Caroline, dear, what had you so busy all day that you had to decline my dinner invitation?" Leaning back in his chair with his hand behind his head, he focused full attention on Caroline. "Or was that an excuse to avoid me?"

"My, you do think a lot about yourself, don't you?" biting into her second slice of pizza. "Not that it's any of your business, but if you must know, I was job hunting.

Logan felt a tiny pinch of guilt, for he knew Maranda had engaged for his help in assisting Caroline out of her predicament. "I take it you had no luck?"

"Nope." Caroline shook her head, placing her wine glass back onto the table, licking the red stains off her lips innocently, yet not realizing it could land her in so much trouble.

"Oh, I'm sorry."

"Why?" she lifted her head high, staring at Logan. "It's not as though you could have done anything about it."

There it was again, that feeling of guilt, wondering what she would think if she knew it was for his selfish reasons that he chose not to help. Would she think any less of him for doing so?

"Besides," she leaned across the table, placing her chin in her hands, "I can always take you up on your offer."

"I like the way you think." He nodded slightly, agreeing, "A little insulted for being the second choice, but what the hack."

"You like games, Logan?" Changing her tone, she plated her fingers and leaned forward.

"Who doesn't?"

"I wonder. How long has it been?" Enticingly biting at her bottom lip.

"How long has what been?"

"Come on, handsome, keep up." Her gaze was long and intense. "How long has it been since a woman fucked the life out of you?"

Logan cleared his throat. "Too long, are you offering?" he could almost hear his heart pounding against his chest.

"I bet I can make you cum without ever having laid a finger on you." Caroline slid her fingers slowly on the tabletop, walking around until she stood before Logan.

"Can you now?" He sat back in his chair, intrigued, mask his face.

"I guess it's no longer a matter of if you'd like to play, but more a matter of if you could play?" Her intense eye contact told him how confident she was in her seducing game.

"Am I at least allowed to ask the game's name?" He asked with a willing, enthusiastic grin.

"It's a wicked, wicked, wicked game." She leaned over and whispered into Logan's ear before biting at his earlobes.

Logan cleared his throat again. "Are there any rules to this wicked game, or do we make the rules up as we go?"

"Rules, Logan, are straightforward." She spoke slowly and with a soft, erotic voice. "All you have to do is demand something from me, whatever it may be. I'll have no choice but to comply, but keep in mind no touching, licking," she ran her tongue slowly over the top of her lip. "Or tasting. Stick to the rules, Logan, and we'll have no problem, and maybe I'll even let you play again."

"Anything?" his eyes held a twinkle of mischief.

"That's the game, handsome." She nodded in agreement.

The game had not yet started, and already he could feel the blood rushing throughout his veins. "What if I were to ask what's under your towel?" His eyes met hers before dropping to the towel that hugged her body.

"Come now, Logan, you don't strike me as the shy type. Life is too short to be anything but happy, and sometimes you have to bend the rules a little and take certain risks." She slides a finger over his chest. "Makes things that more exciting." She teased. "And excitement is what you're looking for, is it not?" Lifting her arms above her head, Caroline allowed the towel to drop to the floor. "See now, all you had to do was ask."

"Logan stared at Caroline in awe with a yawning look that seemed to cover his face instantly at the sight of her naked body. Well, within hand's reach away from him. "Fucking amazing. I swear, Caroline, you have all the right curves in all the right places." He shifted uneasily in his seat with a wicked glint in his eyes.

"I'm glad you feel that way, Logan, because now it's my turn." Taking his hand, she led him up the stairs into her bedroom. "Please sit. Make yourself comfortable; she offers him a chair." Caroline excused herself, returning a few minutes later. "Are you scared of me, Logan?"

Logan's eyes dropped to the duck tape roll in her hands. "I don't know, should I be?"

"You shouldn't be playing with fire if you can't handle the heat, Logan." She bound his hands to the chair. "A little something just in case you're tempted to break any rules." Sitting on Logan's lap, Caroline threw herself against him, rotating her hips slowly. "You like excitement, don't you?" She whispered, climbing onto the bed with her legs spread wide and pressing her feet onto Logan's lap. Caroline pulled her pink vibrator out from under the pillow.

"Fuck!" Taking deep breaths, Logan's eyes held nothing but a deep desire to break every rule of this tormenting game.

"Do you want me, Logan?"

"Oh, you have no idea how much. I want you so badly right now." He whispered with a deep, greedy voice, watching her every movement through gleaming eyes.

"I bet you want to touch me, don't you? Maybe even lick and suck me too?" Caroline tossed her hips forward as she placed the full nine-inch vibrating dildo into her wet, waiting, and ready pussy.

Logan's panting could be heard throughout the entire bedroom as he tugged at his hand.

"You want to eat me, don't you?" Sliding the dildo in and out of her pussy, bringing it up to her clit for a few seconds. Before pushing the vibrator back inside her opening again. "Would you like to see me cum for you, Logan?" Bringing her hips forward, Caroline pushed the dildo harder, and with a faster pace, feeling the rush of excitement, she pulled the vibrator out, spraying the fluid jet onto the bed and Logan's clothes.

"Untie me, now," he ordered, jerking at his hands.

Caroline followed his eyes to his still erected but wet thighs. "Seems your boy has no control." Using a pair of scissors to free Logan's hand. "I need a shower, Logan. You can find your way out the same way you got in." Her tone and body language told a completely different story from a few moments ago, telling Logan that this game was over whether or not he liked it.

CHAPTER ELEVEN

"Logan, can you please watch the girls? I need to run some earrings. Logan, Logan!"

"Huh," Logan looked up from behind his desk. "I'm sorry dear, what did you say?"

Emma stood at the doorway and folded her arms, staring at her husband as heat rushed through her body. "I have been calling you for five minutes, Logan!"

"I'm sorry, love, my mind was preoccupied." Logan rocked back in the big leather chair, twiddling a pen.

"Must be pretty darn important." Emma's eyes dropped to the unopened file in front of her husband. "Given that I've been standing here for the past five minutes, and you've managed to look right past me not once but a couple of times!"

"Is there a point to all this, Emma, or did you just want to stand there all day shouting at me?" Raising his voice louder than he probably should have.

"You know what, Logan! Never mind, I'll take the kids with me!" Emma stormed out, slamming the door behind her. "I swear you can be so useless at times."

Logan got to his feet and flung the pen, hauling it across the room, watching as it hit the wall and rolled a few inches before coming to a halt in front of the doorway. He slammed his fist on the desk. "Fuck!" He yelled out, placing one hand in his pocket. He paced the office floor, walked over to the bar, poured himself a glass of scotch, and twisted his face as the warm liquid slid smoothly down his throat.

(What *in* the hell is going on?) Asking himself the silent question. Lighting a cigar, Logan stood at the corner of the window and watched as Emma bundled the girls into the backseat of the car before walking to the driver's side. Logan watched until the red Toyota turned the corner and disappeared.

It had been three days since his return home, yet getting Caroline off his mind was nearly impossible. He ate, slept, and breadth her name. Caroline had managed to sneak into every crease and corner of his mind and heart. It would seem. Puffing the last smoke, Logan flicks the cigarette butt out the window.

He had promised never to call or message Caroline from the home phone in town where Emma and the girls lived, but for some reason, this particular task turned out to be much more complex than he had expected.

Placing his left hand into his pocket, Logan stood staring at the phone on the desk. "Bloody hell," he walked over and picked the receiver up, dialing Caroline's number. What harm could it do after all? Neither Emma nor the kids were home, and he needed to hear Caroline's voice badly. Leaving no doubt in his mind that Caroline and her wicked tormenting games indeed smote him.

(Hi, I can't come to the phone right now, but if you leave your name and number, I'll get back to you.)

"Where in the hell could she be!" slamming the receiver down, Logan paced the office floor again.

"Hi, Maranda. I'm trying to get in touch with Caroline. Do you, by any chance, know where she is?"

"Have you tried her cell number?" the voice on the other end of the speaker conveyed back to his ear.

"No, I don't have it. Send it to me," he ordered

"I don't know, Logan." A long pause took over. "If Caroline wanted you to have her number, she would have given it to you. I'll need to seek her permission first."

"For heaven's sake, Maranda," he sighs. "It's her phone number, not her bloody PIN."

"I'll do anything for you, Logan, but Caroline is struggling. You should know that. With her marriage, losing her job, the bank coming down on her, and everything else going on in her life, she doesn't need anything more added to her plate. I love you to the ends of the earth, big brother. You know that, but when I asked you to be there for her. I meant to help her get a job, not what I'm seeing unfolding in front of my eyes right now."

"What does any of this have to do with Caroline's number, Maranda? You women always seem to make a mountain out of a hill." He scolded.

Maranda groaned, which Logan could hear from the receiver's end. "Long story short, Logan, you're married. This is not good for either of you. It's not a healthy relationship, and I can't stand by and watch you throw your whole life away for a mere fling, keeping in mind that I care just as much for Caroline as I do you. My advice. End it now, Logan. End it before it goes any further. I assure you that this love triangle wouldn't end well for the three parties involved." A long pause. "Logan, are you there?"

"I'm here."

"I'm only trying to do what is best for both you and Caroline."

"I can take care of myself, Maranda. Thanks for nothing." Logan was exasperated and slammed the receiver down.

Fuck this crap. Grabbing a pen and piece of paper, Logan jotted down a short note explaining to Emma that something had come up at the office and he had to attend an emergency meeting. Sticking the message on the refrigerator door, he snatched his keys from the counter and scampered for the door.

It will be a long, tiring drive, but he should be at Caroline's by nightfall if he leaves now. Logan peered into the review mirror and waited until it was safe to pull onto the highway lane. Turning the music up, his thumb finger beat on the hard steering wheel while his right hand dangled out the window as excitement rushed through his veins at the thought of Caroline in his arms tonight.

Two hours later, Logan drove into Caroline's driveway. Pulling his van to a halt, he climbed out and indulged himself in a cigarette as the anxiety of what the night holds took him over. Walking back to the van, Logan took a much-needed deep breath before taking up the bottle of wine and red rose he had stopped to purchase on his drive here.

Caroline strolled into the room, wiping the water drifting down her body, "Geez! Logan!" her startled eyes met his. Quickly, she draped the towel around her nakedness. Panting, she pressed her hand to her chest. "You really need to stop doing that."

"You were at home the whole day?" Logan lay on the bed, his head propped against his elbow. He indulged his eyes as he watched Caroline's every enticing move.

"I don't see how that's any of your business, Logan!" she walked to the vanity, brushing her long, wavy hair. "Out of curiosity, how did you get into my house this time?" she turned and waved the hairbrush at him. "And don't tell me I forgot the keys in the door again." She said, giving him a scolding look. "Because I know I didn't."

"I duplicated your house key."

"You did, what!" Caroline's eyes widened, flaring at him. "How dare you, Logan? What gives you the right!"

"This," Logan sneaked up behind, grabbing a handful of Caroline's hair. He pulled her head backward. "This gives me that right." He ran a finger slowly down her neckline, whispering into her ear. "The way your body responds to mine, the way my body responds to yours."

Taking her hand, he pressed it to his already erected cock. "I want you, Caroline. I want you for Breakfast, lunch, dinner, and dessert. Yes, I'm that greedy." his deep, husky tone was soft yet at the same time demanding.

Breathing heavily, Caroline could feel the rise and fall of her chest. "A man like you, Logan. I can see you have a healthy appetite." Caroline span, putting her self-defense skills into full action, clamping a pair of handcuffs around Logan's wrist to the tall post bed behind him. "Breakfast, lunch, dinner, and dessert, huh? But believe me when I tell you, Logan, you're not ready for the main course. Not yet, anyway."

A sly, naughty smile curved the corner of her lips. "You'll find I'm assorted, unlike any other girl you've grown used and accustomed to. I'm the kind of woman who likes preparing her own meals, and Logan," she took extreme pleasure, sliding her hand slowly between his thighs and roughly grabbing his eagerly awaiting stiff cock. "I think my meal is just about ready." She whispered with firm, intense eye contact. The tip of her nose grazed slightly against his.

Impressed and intrigued by her sudden, unexpected moves, Logan stood helplessly with both hands bound yet again, having no choice but to give in to her dominance. She was right about one thing in particular. She was like no other he had ever had. He listened as the buttons of his shirt fell to the floor one after the other yet again.

"I'm the kind that likes ripping her gifts open." She pushed the shirt over his shoulders, leaving it to hang loose.

"Drink." She put the bottle of wine in his mouth; Caroline licked the fallen drips from his chest, gliding her tongue up to his lips. "Umm, taste better this way." Lightly sinking her teeth, she pulled gently at his bottom lips. "Do you want me, Logan? I bet you can't wait to feel my lips around your hard, hard cock. Licking, sucking, sliding as far back down into my throat." Her fingers worked on his belt, unzipping his pants. She allowed it to drop to the floor. The longing in Logan's eyes was like adrenaline for Caroline. "You'll like that, won't you?"

"Oh, fuck yes. I'd love it." Logan's eyes drifted shut, unable to focus on much else except for Caroline's gentle strokes on his cock that was shamelessly ready to burst.

"I knew you would, Logan, but it's like I conveyed to you a few days back. There will be no licking, touching, or sucking. However, I feel generous tonight. And because you've been such a good sportsman and have obeyed the rules thus far, I'm willing to bend the rules a little." She nibbled his earlobe. "Tell me, Logan. Would you like that?"

"You know I would." Unabashed by her seduction, he was overcome by the desire to have her. he jerked at the handcuffs with an impatient rumble. "Let me loose, Caroline."

"And what if I don't?" she teased.

His tongue darted out and slid across his lips. "Then, you'll have to pay the ultimate price." He tugged at his hands again.

"Seems to me you're in no position to make demands or treats. Big boy." She jerked at his cocked aggressively. My game, Logan. My rules." Slightly brushing her lips against his, feeling the tension building in his body Caroline stood stroking his cock back and forth until she felt the built-up of his full potential.

Descending to her knees, she opened her mouth and guided most of the volcanic eruption into her mouth. In contrast, some white milky substance remains scattered throughout her face and leaked to her chest.

"Oh, good heavens, Caroline. You're steering me insane." His jaw tightens as he stands, watching Caroline scoop his liquid off her chest and suck the cum off her fingers. He had never been so darn turned on as he is now. He wanted her badly. But he knew better, and he'd have his way when the time was right.

CHAPTER TWELVE

John tapped on the door before opening it. "We need to talk, Logan." his hand clenched at the door knob.

"Not now." Logan turned the page and continued reading through the file before him, not bothering to look up.

Slamming the door behind him, John bolted into the office. "No, now!" he shouted.

Taking a while before responding, Logan's eyes bounced from John to the open blinds through the glass wall to his office. "Unlike you, John." Logan dropped the pen, glaring at John, and plated his fingers under his chin. "Some of us have to work for a living."

"Don't feed me that crap, Logan!" leaning forward. He slammed his fist on the desk. "My three-month suspension ended two weeks ago. I need my job back, Logan, yesterday."

Logan got to his feet, adjusting his tie. He walked over to the glass wall, shutting off the blinds, allowing them some privacy from the glaring eyes outside.

"I'll sue, Logan. If I don't get word from the company within the next few days, I'll sue this company for every cent it's got!" Pushing his hand into his pocket, he paced the large office from one end of the wall to the next, fidgeting.

"Careful now, John, you're starting to sound desperate." Logan turned, holding a glass of whiskey he had just poured out to John. "Drink?" he offered

John snatched the drink from Logan's hand, gulping it down. "I'm not kidding, Logan. I mean every single word of what I said." Slamming the empty glass on the desk, he began to pace the office floor again, pausing to look at Logan. "Well?"

"Well, had you given me a chance?" Logan walked back and sat down behind his desk. I was just about to call and inform you that you are to report for duty on Monday morning." Signing the document on the desk, Logan closed the file, handing it over to John.

He pulled it back when John reached over. "Don't screw this one up, John, for as much as you are a valuable asset to my company, I would not hesitate to fire your ass the next time it happens," Logan assured him before passing the document over to him.

Clutching the file towards his chest with both hands "Thanks, man, and I am sorry. I can assure you it will not happen again."

"That's a promise I'll be holding you to, John. Now, if you don't mind, I've got a lot to get done."

"Okay, okay, I can take a hint John walked towards the door. "Out of curiosity, Logan, have you fucked my wife yet?" he stopped and turned around. "Hey, I'm sorry, man, but I have to ask. With the money lender down my throat and all." He gestured with his hand

"Forgive me if I'm wrong here, but I don't see how any of what Caroline and I do is your business." Logan looked up from his desk, shocked but not surprised by John's question.

"Now, see there..." John pointed the file at Logan, walking back into the office. "Aside from the fact that we got a wager riding on this, you seem to be forgetting the most crucial factor.

"And what might that be?" Logan replied in a calm, collective tone

"Caroline is my wife." He dragged his words to ensure Logan understood what he was saying.

"Your wife?" Logan looked a little bemused. "You know, John, I don't think you even comprehend the word wife.

"Coming from a married man, who's fucking another man's wife, pray to tell Logan since you're the expert on wives; please explain it to me?" John lashed out in a sarcastic tone.

"Let me make myself abundantly clear to you, John. I refuse to be an accomplice in this ruthless, insensitive, heartless game you seem to be playing. Plain and simple, the bet is off."

John gave Logan a slight nod with a glint of annoyance. "You don't just decide to call off a wager in the middle of a game, Logan, a fundamental rule to gambling. Things like that could have major repercussions. One might even end up losing more than they originally bargained for. You never try to out-gamble a gambler."

"Are you really that heartless?" Logan rocked back in his chair, tapping his finger on the desk; his jaw bone tightened, giving John a cold stare. "Haven't you done enough to this woman without causing any more havoc in her life?" Logan opened the top drawer of his desk. "Either way, I had anticipated this would be your reaction." Logan slid the check he was holding over to John. "I've always been a man of my word, John, and that's not going to change for you or anyone else. After today, I want no part of you aside for when it comes down to business. Do I make myself clear?"

"Loud and clear, Mr. Forrester, business only." Focusing more on the paper in his hand, John slid the check into the folder and proceeded toward the door. "Out of curiosity, what made you change your mind?" he looked back at Logan, letting out a loud, obnoxious laugh. "Don't tell me you've fallen for the bitch?" tilting his head. "You have, haven't you?" closing the door, Logan could hear the echoes of John's laughter fading off in the distance.

"Hello, Caroline. Is everything okay?"

"Logan, I'm sorry for interrupting you while you're at work. I was supposed to meet Maranda at the club, but she didn't, and now my car won't start." She sighed. "I don't know who else to call." She exasperated.

"Stay where you are. I'm coming to get you."

"I hate how he throws order around as he owns me." Caroline wrapped her hands around her shoulder as the chill of the night's air started to creep in. Her eyes wandered into the beauty of her Surroundings.

Malabar was a small-town countryside where the roads came to an end to white sandy beaches and baby blue skies that kissed the blue, green ocean waters by day, then gradually turned to bright orange whenever the moon would peep out at night time, where coconut tree branches would often be caught dancing to the tune of the windy breeze and the crashing of the waves against the rocky slopes, which over the years had started taking piece by piece of what used to be twin sister peek mountains that now stood side by side of what's left and could barely be referred to as hills now.

The old Catholic Church, a building that stood at the beachfront for over a century, was a historical sight for newcomers and visitors alike.

Few houses overlooked the beachfront, although most were spaced apart along the roadside with white picket fences and well-groomed lawns.

The villages were often friendly and welcoming; however, it was a place where everyone knew everyone. Caroline couldn't quite tell if that was a good thing or bad. And recently found herself to be the center of attention almost everywhere she went. Tried as she may to ignore the gossip, she had to admit it did get to her some. The fake smile she managed to put on every morning before leaving the house has now become a permanent part of her morning makeup.

Lifting her hand to protect her eyes from the beaming bright light that headed towards her, Caroline closed her eyes before the vehicle stopped.

"Did I not tell you to wait where you were?" Logan's angry voice shouted, "Do you know the panic that went through my mind when I saw the car, but you were nowhere to be found?" He scolded. "You could have at least taken your phone with you."

Caroline lounged next to Logan with folded arms and pouted silently.

"Put your seatbelt on." He ordered as he pulled the van back onto the road, silence filling the air. Logan cast a sideward glance at Caroline. "I'm sorry I yelled at you,"

"O my god, this is like one of my favorite songs." Reaching out, she turned the music up, rocking her head back and forth. Caroline sang word for word, snapping her fingers to the beat of the music. "Believe me when I tell you, Logan, I'm a big girl quite capable of caring for myself." She continues singing

"And now you don't have to anymore. That's what I'm here for." He glanced in her direction.

"Sing along with me."

"I will not." He honked his horn at the two women who crossed the road without looking left or right. "Stupid kids these days," he muttered.

"Come on, Logan, try it. It'll be fun."

"What's fun for me is watching your skirt slide further with each move you make." Giving Caroline a devilish grin.

"Now." Caroline licked her lips, reaching for his pants.

"What are you doing?" He tightens his grip on the steering wheel, trying to focus on the roads ahead.

"Come on now. You're a big boy."

"As much as I would love to play with you right now, Bunny, I need to focus on my task." Feeling the warmness of Caroline's mouth engulfed his cock.

"Focus on the road if you value your life, Logan."

"Oh fuck, yes." Inhaling deeply, Logan anchored himself, grabbing Caroline's ponytail with one hand. He pressed her head down as her tongue worked magic on his cock. "Holy crap!" between the explosion of his cock and having to swing away from the black Corolla heading straight into them, Logan couldn't quite tell which excited him more.

Caroline lifted her head slowly, licking at her lips.

Logan pulled the van into Caroline's driveway and switched the ignition off. Climbing out, he walked her to the door.

"Well, I can't say it hasn't been an entertaining night." Caroline opened the door. "Thanks, Logan, for all your troubles."

Logan grabbed the side of Caroline's head, running his finger down her cheek. The longing in his eyes could seduce any woman to hell and back. "I want you so fucking bad." Speaking softly, his lips brushed against her face before finding their way to her mouth, kissing her with hunger. Pushing the door shut with his foot, Logan guided Caroline up the stairs while peeling her clothes off piece by piece.

Throwing her onto the bed, he peeled at his shirt. "It's my turn, love. The only difference is my game, my rules, and this time, sweetheart." Feeling the rise and fall of Caroline's heavy breathing, Logan clamped her wrist to the bed, pressing his naked body on top of hers. "This time, my love, there will be touching." He glides his hand slowly down her nude body, teasing her. "There will be kissing." Sliding his tongue past her lips, he looked at her now glassy eyes. "There will be sucking." He whispered into her ear. "And there will, be fucking." His eyes held nothing but desperation as his hand traveled down her body and lingered up her leg to the soft wet moisture of her already leaking pussy.

Caroline closed her eyes, pulling her legs together.

"Now, my love, you need to obey the rules. Wasn't those your words?" Logan parted her legs, trailing his tongue down her chest finding her light brown nipples and sucking until they stood hard and firm beneath his tongue. "You will beg for me to take you, Caroline." he teased as his mouth found its way down her tummy and between the small v of her inner thigh. Caroline lifted her hips to meet his eagerly awaiting lips. Soft moans escaped her throat, grasping at Logan, wanting more of what he was doing.

Logan fed his way back to her, breastfeeding greedily as Caroline's body squirmed beneath his, inviting him in. "Not yet, my love, not until I hear those two words from you." Nothing about his lovemaking was gentle at this point.

"Please, Logan,"

Her pleas only made Logan's aggression more adamant. "Words Caroline." Lifting himself just enough to see her face, he allowed the tip of his cock to gently massage her clit.

Caroline tosses her hips forward, wanting all of him. "Now Logan, please now." pulling his body towards hers.

"Come now, Caroline. You shouldn't play with fire if you can't stand the heat." He continued to taunt her.

"Fuck me, Logan, fuck me now." Digging her nails into his back as the entire length of his cock entered her.

"No marks, darling." He clamped her hand onto the bed, restricting her.

His soft murmurs into Caroline's ear reminded her that Logan was like a hot meal she could order and enjoy at a restaurant but could not take home. He was both dinner and dessert, but never could he be breakfast.

Moving her hips in slow round movements, she thus her hips upward, ready to take all of him.

"Answer the phone, Darling." Logan looked at John's name as it appeared on Caroline's phone screen.

Caroline nodded, "I can't..." her voice breaking.

"Answer it, darling, or I will." Logan demanded, "I don't play nice, Caroline. You're mine. No one touches you but me. I want him to hear you scream out my name," He ordered her.

Caroline's hand fumbled with the phone, sliding at the screen. "Jo... John." Once again, her voice broke.

Breathing heavily as Logan slammed his shaft inside her, she gave out an unexpected scream, dropping the phone to the floor. His hard cock grind slowly at first, then quickly until both could hold back no more. Caroline could feel herself and Logan explode simultaneously, screaming his name out with pure pleasure.

"Caroline, are you okay?" John's voice called out through the speaker.

Logan smiled slyly, kissing Caroline's forehead. He rolled off her, pulling her onto his chest. "You will always remember what I feel like inside you, Caroline, because it will be the only cock that will be entering into you from here onward." stroking her cheek. "You are an amazing lover."

CHAPTER THIRTEEN

"Bastard John screamed, "How dear him?"

"Calm down, John. What did Logan do that has you so angry?" Clair poured a glass of whiskey, walking over to John. "Take this. You look like you need it more than I do."

Unable to sit, John got to his feet again. "The dirty little whore thinks she can betray me and get away with it."

"Okay, now I'm confused. You're speaking in riddles here." Clair sat on the gold-colored couch and pulled her feet beneath her. She made herself comfortable. It would seem that she was in for a long night; for she had grown so used to John and his ranting and ravings that she knew pretty well what was expected by now. "Correct me if I'm wrong here, John, but won't you be the one who wanted out of this marriage in the first place."

Pacing back and forth, John pelts the glass of whiskey against the wall, ignoring Clair's remark. "They will not get away with this if it means I have to fuck Emma myself." He trembled with outrage, placing the open bottle of whiskey in his mouth. "You will see mark my words, Clair. My name will feel like salt on his tongue when I'm through with Logan. Taking a long drink, he slammed the bottle on the table.

"Come sit next to me." Clair patted the space next to her, gently rubbing John's shoulders. "You're tense, Darling. Try calming yourself a bit and allow me to distress you." She kissed his neck.

"Not now, Clair." Lifting his hand, he pushed her away. "I'm not in the mood."

More hurt than angry, Clair got to her feet. "That's the problem right there, John. Recently, you never seem to be in the mood for anything." She yelled, "No wonder that whore of a wife is fucking another man. I think you were never brave enough to satisfy her needs."

John scampered over, grabbing Clair's throat and throwing her to the couch. He pinned her down. "Don't you ever speak ill of my wife again!" Giving her a cold, angry stare with bulgy eyes. "Not ever!" Squeezing at her neck

"Get your god darn hands off me." Clair pushed at him, holding her throat, coughing. "Get the fuck out of my house, John!" she yelled.

"I don't need this fucking crap out of you, fuck you, Clair!" Grabbing his jacket in a rage "Don't wait up for me tonight."

Emma threw her robe on, almost running towards the door, pausing briefly to look at the clock on the wall at 2.15 a.m. Who in the hell could that be at this god-forsaken time of the morning, peering through the peephole of her front door?

"John," Lifting the latch, Emma opened the door, inviting him in. "Is everything okay, John? How is Logan? Is he okay?" Panic ran through her, curious as to what could have brought John out at this time of the night.

"Offer me a drink, Emma, and while you're at it, you should also have yourself one."

"I don't think so, John, and I don't drink." Emma looked at him. He was drunk and reeked of alcohol. Offering him more would probably invite trouble and make matters worse. He had something on his chest that he desperately needed to get out. "Please have a seat." Gesturing to the couch.

John passed his hand through his hair, looking at Emma. He obeyed like a puppy would.

Emma sat opposite him, leaning back. She crossed one leg over the other. "Now tell me, what is so important you couldn't wait till morning?"

John got to his feet. "Do you know where your husband is, Emma, at this very moment?"

"I'm guessing in bed, sleeping. It is after two in the morning, John."

"Yes, but do you know who's the bed?"

"Is there a point to all this, John? I am pretty tired and must be up early in the morning."

John rubbed the back of his neck, twisting it from side to side. "I'm sorry to be the bearer of bad news, Emma. But as we speak, your husband and my wife are wrapped tightly in each other's arms."

Emma sat motionless for what seemed like an eternity

"I am so sorry, Em..."

"Tell me, John," Emma interrupted. "What exactly did you expect by revealing this information to me?" she got up and walked a short distance from the couch. "That I'd be so hurt and angry, I'd rush to your arms and fuck you to get back at Logan? Revenge on your wife for fucking with another man? Revenge on Logan for fucking your wife?" "Or maybe it's just that the hurt and betrayal of finding out just drives you crazy, knowing that Caroline had the guts to move on after what you did to her." Emma gave a sarcastic laugh. "Yes, I know, John. Everybody knows what a despicable, sorry excuse for a man you are."

John stood with a confused look written across his face. "Emma, did you hear what I said? Do you understand that at this very moment, your husband is in the arms of another woman?" John repeated himself.

"Don't you ever stand there for a minute and justify what you're doing for my good because we both know that you are doing it for selfish reasons and nothing more. Because John has never been known to think of anyone else except for himself." Emma looked at him with scorn. "Know this, John, I will not now nor will I ever stand by and allow anyone to come in between me and my family!" She walks towards the door, holding it open for him. "On another note, you are a shameless man, John, and tonight you just proved it." Emma stood as he brushed past her. "I pray for your sake, John, that Logan never comes to find out about this."

Closing the door, Emma inhaled deeply. Could any of this be true? It seems that God has been listening to me and praying after all. Breathing a sigh, she turned the lights off and returned to bed feeling like the world's weight had lifted off her shoulders.

CHAPTER FOURTEEN

Caroline ignored the young man's unpleasant comment and continued wiping the counter. "Jim, could you please take care of this one." Rolling her eyes as she walked away.

"No worries, love." Jim winked at her, trying to hide the humour on his face. He had gotten used to rescuing her from drunks, not so drunk or simply admirers. Caroline had managed to land herself a job at the club and, as it turned out (The Night Club) had pulled more customers in the past two weeks than in the past months. "So, what will it be, Tim?" Jim waited for a response

"The Doll behind the counter, please." displaying a wide, obnoxious grin that covered his face from ear to ear.

Jim turned his head, following the man's eyes. Placing his hand on the counter, he leaned forward. "I'd like to, mate," Tilting his head to one side, "But you see, the thing is, that Doll is not for sale. Howler when you're ready to order." He patted the counter before pouring some tequila shots for another waiting customer.

"Six beers for table nine." Caroline rushed over to the freezer. Grabbing the beers, she popped them open one by one.

"Wow! What an ass!" the young man reached over the counter, grabbing Caroline's hand. "How about a kiss, Darling?"

"Get your filthy hands off her," A hand clamped over Tim's. "Now!"

Caroline lifted her head to the sound of the familiar voice

"What are you, her bodyguard?" taking no heed to the warning.

Twisting Tim's hand behind his back to breaking point, "I said, get your hands off her!" Logan's eyes narrowed with a heated, scorching glare. "I'm usually a nice guy, Tim, but don't let that fool you because I can get nasty quickly. Especially when it comes down to the woman I love." Jerking Tim towards the door, "Get out of here!"

Caroline's eyes met Logan's. Did he say what she thought he did? Maybe she heard wrong; the music was banging after all.

"Come with me, now!" Logan grabs hold of Caroline's hand, dragging her along with him.

"Logan, I can't leave now. I'm working." Almost running to keep up with him. "Let go of my hand." Jerking her hand away, she straightens her clothes.

"Is everything okay here?" Jim stepped in front of Caroline.

"It's okay, Jim, I'll take care of this," assuring him she had things under control.

"You sure about that?"

"I'm sure." Offering the older man, a shaky smile.

"At least take this in private." He led them into his office.

"Thanks, Jim." Caroline hugged herself as she walked into the room with Logan tailing close behind.

"What are you doing in a place like this, Caroline?"

"Well, I was working, or so I thought." She replied with light sarcasm

Logan sighs heavily, pushing the door shut behind him. "Is there something you lack that I don't know of? Have I failed you in any way?" looking at her with questioning eyes, a long silence took over. "What are you doing here, Caroline? I take care of your every need, your every want." He walked up to her. "I take care of you," lifting her chin. "You don't need this kind of drama in your life."

She flinched and pulled away. “And I need you. A married man?” Turning away from him, “You think that’s not drama.” Her voice was brittle and breaking.

“What are you talking about? I don’t understand where all this is coming from?”

“You know what, Logan? I can’t deal with this right now!” she said, throwing her hands up and surrendering.

“You knew this when we started, Caroline. I’ve been upfront with you, and you agreed to it.” His eyes followed her movement attentively.

“You don’t belong to me, Logan, and the faster I come to terms with our situation, the better off I’ll be.”

“Listen to me, Sweetheart.” He cupped her face with both hands. “You are my,”

“What! What am I, Logan?” shoving him away from her. “Tell me?” She pushed at his chest again. “Your girlfriend, your mistress, your whore?!” spitting the words out scornfully.

“My lover!” He grabbed her upper arms and shook her back and forth. “My lover, darn it!” he pulled her to his chest, holding her close, not wanting to let her go for fear of losing her.

Knock, Knock, two gentle taps on the door before it opened. “Caroline,”

“Close the fucking door!” Logan shouted angrily.

“I need to go now, Logan,” Caroline murmured.

“Where are you going?”

“Back to work.”

“But I’m not finished with you yet.”

“I must get back to work before losing my job, Logan.

“You are not going back out there, Caroline.” He shouted, jerking her impatiently back towards him.

“And who are you to tell me what I can and can’t do?” giving him a hard, cold, intense stare.

"Your man, that's who I am, and it seems you need to be reminded of that fact." He reached out, sliding his hand to the nape of her neck and pulling her towards him. He sorted her lips with his. "See how quickly your body reacts to mine," he whispered in her ear as his hand unbuttoned the top of her shirt. His hand cups her bare breasts, caressing them. "Tell me now, my love, that you don't know who I am?" he pushed her against the wall, pressing his body weight and pinning her to the wall, rendering her helpless.

"Logan. You can't, not here."

"You talk too much." Covering her mouth with his, Logan's tongue explored the sweet honey nectar of Caroline's mouth. "You are mine and mine only." He slides his hand up her skirt into her panties, rubbing her.

Caroline grabbed his chest, pulling him closer, breathing out of control, hungry with desire.

"I'm going to fuck you, Caroline, first with my fingers, then with my tongue, then with my cock. I want to hear you scream out to me again and again. I want to feel my cock inside you as you shout my name." Logan pushed his leg, parting hers and sliding down before her. He lifted her skirt, pushing two fingers into her. He pulled her hips to his mouth."

Caroline's hands grabbed at the wall for support. She could almost hear the rapid rate of her heartbeat pounding against her chest; she pushed herself forward, "Logan." she whispered in a hushed tone.

"It's good you remember my name, love. Because that's the name you will scream for the rest of your life." He bent her over the desk, unzipped his pants, freed his cock, and impaled his entire length into her. He listened as she screamed out his name again. Caroline rocked back to meet his every movement.

Logan sat on a chair, aggressively pulling her on his lap. "Ride me, baby, ride me hard." He slid his hand around her body while his lips suckled at her nipples. A move that sent her insane and to the brink of orgasm.

Caroline tugged his head toward her neck. “Bite me, Logan. Bite me, please.” She pleaded, engulfed with an exciting burning desire.

Even the feel of her long pink nails digging into his back was an incredible, painful pleasure he had only experienced for the first time in his lovemaking life.

Holding her sweaty body still sitting on his lap, he caressed her to him. “You are quite a wild one, Caroline.” He patted her butt. “Come now, and I think we’ve used Jim’s office well.” He helped her to her feet.

“Oh, crap, my make-up is in a mess.”

“You look beautiful” Logan slapped her ass, hugging her from behind.

“What will Jim say when he sees me looking like this?”

“He’ll say that we made good use of his office,” Logan says with a hint of mischief.

“Ha-ha, not funny, Logan.”

“Come on,” He pinched her nose. “Who cares how you look? To me, you’re beautiful. More so when you’ve been fucked.”

“Oh no, don’t even think about it.” Caroline giggled and backed away.

“Once more.” Pushing her against the wall and sliding her skirt up. “I swear, Caroline, you’ll love the feel of me inside you,” he whispered.

CHAPTER FIFTEEN

Caroline opened the door. A dumbfounded look instantly covered her face as Emma walked past her, looking around the small, cozy living room before making herself comfortable on the sofa.

"Quite comfy." She looked up at her rival. "Come on, dear. Offer me something to drink."

Caroline quietly walked towards the kitchen like a child would when obeying a parent's demand. She returned a short while later with two cups of coffee in hand. "I'm sorry, but I'm out of alcohol."

"I'm sure you need it," Emma says, taking the cup from Caroline's hand. "That reflects badly on my husband or, should I say, your lover?" Lifting her eyebrows, she took in Caroline's response.

A flush crept across Caroline's cheeks, and she looked straight past Emma.

Emma folded her legs; paying close attention to Caroline's every move. "I'll have to have a talk with him about that."

Caroline rests her cup on the glass coffee table. "Emma, I..."

"Oh, suck it up, Caroline!" taking a sip from her coffee. "Don't ever apologize for taking whatever means necessary you see fit when trying to survive. Oh, bloody hell!" Emma pulled her handbag towards her, pulling a small silver flask out. She opened the cap, poured some white liquid into her cup, and then did the same to Caroline's. "Now, this is a good cup of coffee." She announced, lifting the cup to her mouth.

"Women like us, Caroline, we don't play nice. We have the guts to go after what we want even if it means playing dirty and admirably so, we somehow always manage to get the job done, whatever means necessary." She brought herself closer to the sofa's edge and leaned towards Caroline. "Apologizing is for the weak, a quality we both seem to lack. It's considered a sign of weakness in my book, and I unquestionably would not have my replacement being anything but the bitch I saw when I first walked through that door."

"Okay, hold up there one minute." Holding her hands outward. "I don't mean to be rude here, but women like us? Replacement?" Caroline replied in a sharp tone. "I have no intention of taking your place, Emma, and I most certainly have no intentions of being anyone's replacement. That you can take to the bank with you."

"See, now that's the bitch I was talking about. Feisty and not afraid to speak up in her defense."

"Why would I want to defend myself? I will admit that what Logan and I did was wrong, but had you fulfilled your bedroom duties in the first place, Logan would not have to be prowling mine, making it into his regular playground. So... Either join in and make it a threesome or step aside because I will not stop fucking your man." Caroline reclined in her chair. "Outside of that, if you have any more concerns, I suggest you pick it up with your husband."

Emma calmly laid back on the sofa. Putting her feet up, she closed her eyes. "Caroline, if the situation were reversed, I'd probably say the same thing."

"Is there a point to all this, Emma? Because looking in from the outside, it's clear that you have absolutely no problem with Logan and I doing each other?"

“Must be exciting, huh? Being with a married man. The thrill of a forbidden fruit.”

“Yes, as a matter of fact, it is. Extremely so.”

Emma looked a little hurt at that point but tried her best to shield her emotions. “Has he ever fucked you here, on this sofa? She looked down, passing her hand on the soft fabric. Please don’t lie to me because I can smell him.”

“Why are you doing this to yourself, Emma?”

“Answer me, Caroline. I need to know.”

“Yes.” Caroline folded her arms, staring at Emma, unable to comprehend her reasons.

“How many times?” her voice calm and emotionless

“A few too many.”

“What about on the steps?” casting her eyes over the staircase.

“Emma...”

“Answer my questions,” raising her voice a bit. “Please... her tone died down again.

“Yes, Emma,” Caroline crossed her hand over her chest. “On the stairs, the sofa, the kitchen counter, the corridor against the wall in the bedroom.”

Emma gave a sad, withdrawn smile. “Sounds like my Logan loves excitement. It never really was much of the bedroom kind.

Is there anything else you’ll like to know, like who does more of the fucking, for instance?”

“I think I already know the answer to that question. Your eyes tell a story. Do you like kids, Caroline?”

“What?” I was caught off guard by the sudden shift in conversation.

“It’s a simple yes or no question. Do you like kids?”

“Well, I’ve never really given it much thought, but I guess I would want to someday. I don’t see how any of this is relevant, though.”

“You will, and in time to come, everything will make perfect sense to you.”

To Caroline, Emma's eyes held a somewhat sad and far away withdrawn look.

"I'm going to ask you probably what might be the most important question yet, Caroline, and I want you to be honest about your reply. You owe me that much."

Caroline could hear the desperation in Emma's voice. Shifting in her seat, she realized how much truth there was to that little statement Emma had made and nodded in agreement.

Emma's eyes pierced Caroline's, holding her gaze. "Do you love my husband, Caroline? Are you in love with Logan?"

"I, I..."

"Let me answer that for you." Emma got to her feet. "It started as a fling, and why the hell not? He's married. The thrill and excitement must send a girl like you wild. No commitment, and why would you want that, only now, coming out of an abusive marriage yourself? Anyone could understand you not wanting to commit. Then there's the need for someone who's there for financial support. But then there's the one thing you did not cater for, something you did not even consider would happen because you made yourself so strong. Building a wall so high that no one dares to come close or even try to break it down. Am I right so far?"

"I have no idea what you're talking about." Caroline looked away, refusing to make eye contact with her rival.

"Well then, let me explain it to you, that wall you build around your heart. The one where you promise never to let anyone in ever again. Logan managed to break it down, sneaking his way in without you even realizing when it happened, so yes, my dear, you are in love with my husband."

"Emma..." Caroline looked at her with concern. "Are you okay?"

"Yes, yes, it's this darn dizziness that happens sometimes. Nothing to worry about. I need to sit for a bit, that's all." Emma made her way back to the sofa.

"I'll get you some water." Caroline rushed into the kitchen.

Emma blinked a few times before opening her eyes. “How long have I been out?” sitting up, she passed her hands over her face.

Caroline looked at the watch in her hand. “About two hours.” Rubbing her fingers to her forehead, she looked at Emma with great concern

“I should get going.” Emma tried getting to her feet

“You’re in no condition to be driving anywhere, Emma.” Caroline rushed forward, helping her up

“I have to pick the kids up.”

“I’ll call Logan then.”

“No!” Emma's eyes widen, grabbing the phone from Caroline’s hand. “You can’t.”

“Okay, no, Logan.” Caroline sat back down slowly. “Care to tell me what’s going on here then?” Leaning in to better detect.

Emma turned her head away, trying to conceal the instant tears that filled her eyes.

“You speak of replacement; you wanted to know if I was in love with your husband and if I liked kids. If I didn’t know better, I would think you were pleased that someone else is in Logan’s life.”

“Something like that.” biting at her lips, Emma blinked her tears away

“O my good God, Emma?” Caroline's hands covered her mouth, throwing herself backward in the chair. “Does Logan know?” she quietly asked

“No,” Emma shook her head. “I couldn’t bring myself to tell him or the kids.”

“How bad?”

“Bad enough.” Unable to hold her tears back now, they flowed down her cheeks.

“How long?” Caroline asked, unsure if she wanted to know the answer.

“Three months.” Emma wiped her eyes. “So, you see Caroline now that you know, is it making more sense to you now?” grabbing hold of

Caroline's knees. "A mother's biggest and only concern is that if something happened to her, her kids would be well taken care of."

"Do you know what you are asking of me, Emma?" Caroline stared into nothing without blinking.

"Please, Caroline, I'm grasping at straws here. You have no idea how difficult this is for me; each day that passes is one day closer. I have to make sure that everything is put into place. This is a mother pleading for her children's life. All you have to say is yes." Emma pleaded. "And maybe then I can live the rest of my days peacefully. At least say you'll think about it, please. Logan must never come to know of this, Caroline. This is between you and me, okay."

"As much as I disagree with you on keeping this from Logan and the kids. You can trust me; your secret is safe with me." Caroline watched as Emma turned to walk away with teary eyes. "Emma!"

"Yes."

"I just wanted you to know I think what you're doing is one of the bravest, selfless acts I've ever seen." Caroline stood at the doorway, still holding it open. "Please take care of yourself, Emma. It was truly a pleasure meeting someone like you."

"Thanks, I can honestly say the same about you, Caroline," Emma smiled sadly and turned away.

CHAPTER SIXTEEN

Grabbing an apple from the fruit bowl, Caroline sank her teeth into it and ran towards the door like a child would when excited. "Logan, I wasn't expecting you until..." Her words dried up mid-sentence as she watched the apple roll across the floor. "John..." She stumbled a few steps backward. "I wasn't expecting you..."

"Well, I don't have to ask who you expect." The muscle in his Jaw tightens. "I see you wasted no time replacing me, Caroline?" he bolted past her.

"What do you want, John?" ignoring his snarky remark, she followed close behind. "What are you doing here?"

"The last I checked, my dear Caroline, this is my house, minus the fact that you are fucking another man in my bed?" his voice grew thick with anger. "You are still, my fucking wife!"

"Your wife?" crossing her arms, she challenged his gaze. "Well, that's a new one for the books." Letting out a sarcastic laugh. "It's funny how you never considered that fact when we were married.

Feeling the tightness in his muscles, he briefly clenched his hand, closing the gap between himself and her. Reaching over, he sank his fingers into her cheekbones, tilting her head to meet his fierce stare. "You are my wife, Caroline, until the law says otherwise, and believe me when I tell you it's going to stay that way until death do us part!" Jerking her head to the side, "I hope you get what I mean by that, so I'd be mindful of what I do or say in the future if I were you." his scornful laugh echoed throughout the room, licking her cheek, letting her know who was in charge now.

Caroline twisted her mouth, wiping the slime off her face with the back of her palms, feeling disgusted.

"Where is the darn whiskey!" he shouted. "There must be a bottle hiding somewhere?" Slamming the empty cupboard doors impatiently, he looked in her direction. "Isn't that what your new boyfriend drinks? Where is it?"

John was already wasted. It would be in her best interests not to provoke him any further. Placing her pride aside, Caroline decided to play things cool until Logan's arrival, which should not be too long from now. Casting a glance toward the kitchen, she remembered her phone. This was her one chance of getting to it. The rage in John's eyes was like none other she had seen before.

"Where the fuck, are you going?"

"To get you a drink." She answered in a shaky voice, shivering a bit

John grabbed Caroline's hair, pelting her to the couch, feeling the need inside to control her completely. Lifting her hand, Caroline tilted her head to shield her face from his oncoming blows.

"You must think I'm stupid, don't you?" punching her several times before climbing off her. "You think I don't know what you're going to call your stupid little boyfriend?" grinding his teeth, he clenched his jaw, venting anger.

Whimpering, Caroline rolled off the couch, falling face down onto the floor. Struggling, she got on all fours, crawling a short distance away before feeling the impact of John's feet against her ribs, throwing her across the hall and onto the wall.

Folding her arms around her body, Caroline's heart raced with excruciating pain throughout every bone. Gasping for the wall, she climbed to her feet, trying to make her way into the kitchen and away from John.

"Now, see what you made me do." Screaming, refusing to take responsibility for his actions, he paced the room rapidly, sliding his fingers through his hair. "Where are you trying to go again? Haven't you learned your lesson by now?" Grabbing a handful of her hair, John dragged her to the mirror. "Tell me, where is that pretty face of yours now." he continued to taunt her, pulling her head backward. "Bet your boyfriend wouldn't look twice at you now." he spat at her. "You're nothing, Caroline. You're nothing but a dirty little whore!"

Caroline's knees wobbled until finally too weak to hold herself up any longer, her lifeless body crumbled to the floor.

John's head swiftly turned towards the direction of the door. "Just in time, what do you think?" he bent over Caroline, taunting her, pulling a knife from his back pocket. He looked towards the door with nothing but contempt.

"Logan, John's here!" Caroline used the last of her little strength to call out to Logan.

"Why, you little bitch!" he kicked her in the stomach.

"Caroline," Maranda peered through the window after knocking a few times without any response.

"Maranda, what is she doing here? Nosey little bitch." John held Caroline's hands, dragging her into the kitchen and placing his finger to his lips. "Shhh."

(*That's funny, I could have sworn I heard Caroline's voice.*) Maranda walked back to her car. *("Serves you right for not calling first,")* mumbling to herself, noticing Caroline's car parked in the garage. She stopped momentarily, and she turned back, looking at the house. Something didn't feel right. Walking back up the stairs, Maranda lifted the flower pot, looking for a key. (*Not there.*) sliding her fingers above the door ledge. (*Where in God's name could she have* it?) turning the door handle (*That's strange,* it's unlocked), she pushed the door open and peeped inside, bending to pick up the piece of apple from the floor. She noticed the blood splatters on the wall.

Her instinct was right; something was going on here. Maranda listened again. The muffle was coming from the kitchen area. Her eyes followed a blood trail leading her to the kitchen door. Trembling, her hand reached for the doorknob, pushing it open. Though every instinct in her gut had warned her she would not like what was behind the door, nothing had prepared her for the horror she was witnessing now.

"One step closer, and she's dead." John hugged Caroline's body upward with a knife to her neck."

Maranda's eyes widen in terror at seeing Caroline's battered, bloody body. "O my good God!" dropping her handbag to the floor, her hand clamped over her mouth.

"I mean it, Maranda!" John swings Caroline's almost lifeless body, placing the knife closer to her throat. "You know, Maranda, you weren't supposed to witness this, but I guess you're just as good as your brother." Giving Maranda the most menacing laugh she had ever heard.

"John, please..." holding her hand out. "Put the knife down. It's not too late to stop this."

I don't understand women today!" Pressing the knife to Caroline's throat again. "What is it about? Don't come any closer, don't you understand!" he glared at Maranda.

"Okay, I'm not getting any closer, but please, John, let me get Caroline to the hospital. Please look at her. What harm can she do now." Maranda pleaded as tears streamed down her face uncontrollably.

"That's the thing, Maranda. I am looking." He glared at her. "And I have concluded that no one ever has her if I can't." Kissing Caroline's head, he pierced the knife into her back. Releasing Caroline's body, he stood and watched as she fell to the floor.

"No." Maranda held her hand out, screaming as she watched Caroline crumble to the floor like a broken piece of wall. Rushing to Caroline's side, she grabbed the first available towel and placed it over the wound. "Come on, Caroline, stay with me here. You've been through too much in life to give up now."

"John, call a bloody ambulance now!" she shouted, realizing that John was nowhere to be found.

"Don't leave me," Caroline's faint whisper could barely be heard as she reached for Maranda's hand.

"I'm not going to leave you, Hun. I need to get you to a hospital as soon as possible, okay." Tears flowed from Maranda's eyes. "One quick phone call and I'll be right back, promise." Maranda scampered for her handbag.

CHAPTER SEVENTEEN

Maranda hurriedly walked down the hospital corridor. "Logan, where in the hell have you been? I've been trying to reach you for two and a half hours."

"I'm at the hospital, Maranda. Where have you been?" he asked with a strained voice.

"Hospital? I'm at the hospital. How did you find out?" Maranda turned around, searching the hospital corridors.

"I was there when it took place." Logan's voice faded off.

"You were there?" Maranda squinted her eyes. "I don't understand. How could you be there when it took place? I'm a little confused here, Logan. What are you talking about?"

"Emma... Maranda. She took in a little after five this evening," Logan took a deep, prolonged breath. "She's in I.C.U. as we speak."

(Oh no, no, no, this cannot happen on the same day.) "Where are you now, Logan?"

"I'm in the waiting area outside the I.C.U. Department, they would not let me go in to see her."

"Stay there; I'm coming to meet you."

Logan got to his feet and approached his sister.

"How is she?" Maranda gave her brother a comforting hug. "What happened?"

"I can't say except for one minute. She was having a cup of tea. The next, she was lying on the floor."

"Any word from the doctor's yet?"

"No, nothing yet..."

"Was Emma ill, Logan?"

"She hadn't been feeling her best lately, a bit withdrawn and not her usual self, but,"

"I'm looking for a Mr. Logan Forrester." A doctor walked in with his head buried in his white folder.

"I'm Logan," he anxiously stepped forward.

"Ah, hi Logan." reaching for Logan's hand, "My name is Dr Wheeler. Judging from what I'm reading in this file, you already know what's happening here?"

"Why would I?" Logan's eyes narrowed. "I don't understand. If no one has spoken to me, why would I know what's happening?"

Dr. Wheeler lifted his eyes over the open file he was reading, observing Logan's confused reaction. "And he doesn't." Taking a deep breath, Dr. Wheeler closed the file and focused on Logan and Maranda. It seems your wife has been hiding things from you, Mr. Forrester."

"What are you talking about, Doc? Just cut to the chase, will you? What is going on with my wife?"

"I'm not going to sugar-coat this for you, Mr. Forrester. I am not usually the one that handles it. Your wife is dying. She has a disease called glioblastoma. It's a type of cancer that charges its way into the brain tissue diffusely and erratically, making it a surgical nightmare. There's nothing more we can do for her at this stage."

Logan placed his hand over his mouth, slumping to the chair behind him. "How? I mean, she wasn't," his voice faded into silence.

"Emma knew Mr. Forrester. She'd known about it for a while now. I guess she would have her reasons for keeping this news to herself.

Most times, though, they don't want their loved ones to suffer the emotional traumas that this terminal disease can inflict. Don't be too harsh; her intentions were in the right place."

"Come on, Hun." Maranda got to her knees before Logan, "You need to pull yourself together and be strong now more than ever. You can't afford to fall apart. There're still the girls to think about."

"How long?" Logan looked up at Dr. Wheeler

"Hours, days at most." This was the part of his job he hated the most.

"Hours?" Logan's face grew thin and pale.

"Yes, Mr. Forrester, her time is close, and she has regained consciousness. She's asking for you. My advice is don't let her see you like this. Pull yourself together and come in when you think you're ready. Again, I'm sorry. I wish there were something more I could do." Logan sat and watched Dr. Wheeler walk out the door.

Logan looked at Maranda. It was her first time seeing tears in her brother's eyes. Giving him a reassuring look, she reached out to fix his tie. "Come on; I know you can do this. You are much stronger than you think." Patting his shoulders, she wiped the tears from his eyes. "You walk in there and put on the best show of your life. I'll be here right here waiting for you." Faking a smile, her eyes were also filled with tears.

Maranda watched her brother until he was out of sight. (*Holy crap*) she looked at the time she needed to return to Caroline, now hustling down the long corridor. (*Good God*) picking up the pace as she neared the waiting room.

Clearing the corridors, Maranda watched as the doors to the theatre opened and a group of people dressed in green wheeled Caroline out. "Is she okay?"

"Wait here, please. The doctor will be with you shortly." One of the nurses took the time to inform her.

"Thanks." Standing outside the doorway, she peered through the small glass opening at the top of the door, watching as they lifted

Caroline from one bed to the other. Maranda could feel a cold chill in the air. What a day this was turning out to be, one to remember, that was for sure.

"Are you here for?"

"Caroline, yes!" Maranda nervously stepped forward.

"And who are you to the patient?" The doctor enquired

"I'm Maranda, Caroline's best friend."

"I'm sorry, Mam, but I can only divulge Caroline's information to her next of kin."

"Well, knowing that her next of kin is the one who has her in there!" Maranda's raised her voice and pointed towards the room. "I'm the only one she's got, doctor," Tears wield in Maranda's eyes. "So, you might as well tell me what's happening with my friend? Please,"

Shifting his glasses along his nose bridge, he looked at Maranda. "I see. Has this information been passed on to the police yet?"

"It's in the hands of the police as we speak, though my main concern is for Caroline."

"You want the good news first or the bad?"

"I'll leave that up to you." bracing herself for the worst

"Caroline lost much blood. Maranda, is it?"

Maranda just nodded her head.

"She suffered severe lacerations to her head and face. It will take her a while to recover fully if she ever does. Aside from the few broken ribs, cuts, and bruises, your friend should count her blessings that luck was on her side."

"Why do you say that?" Maranda paid close attention to everything that was being said.

"Well, the knife blade missed her spine by less than a centimeter, had it not. Well, I guess you know the answer to that question."

"Thank god." Breathing a sigh of relief, "I was concerned about that."

"Okay, now that the good news is over and done with, it's time for the bad news."

Maranda's head shot up. "That was the good news?" her voice started to break apart.

"I take no pleasure in this; we tried but could do nothing to save the baby."

Maranda's eyes widen. "What did you say?"

"Caroline was five weeks pregnant."

"Does she know?"

"We haven't gotten a chance to break the news to her yet,"

"Doctor Greg, you're needed downstairs now." a slim, dark-skinned nurse peered her head into the room.

"I'll be right there." Turning to Maranda. "Again, I'm sorry. I wish there were something more we could have done for your friend." jotting something down, he tore the page, giving it to Maranda. "Call me if you have any questions, even if it's just to talk, maybe over coffee." Backing away and out the door.

"Wait! Can I see her just for a minute, please?"

"I couldn't say no to you even if I wanted to." Dr. Greg gives her a sympathetic smile. "You'll owe me coffee for this one, I must warn you." He jokingly replied, trying to cheer her up, walking ahead, holding the door open.

"Poor thing," Maranda stared at Caroline feeling helpless. "Is it not amazing how one moment you're happy and vibrant going about your daily activities, and then the next you're lying in a hospital bed fighting for your life?" not expecting a response, she held Caroline's hand in a comforting gesture.

"He pulled a number on her, that much I can tell you."

"Yes, he did. I wonder if she'll ever be able to come out of this her usual variant self again." tears streamed down Maranda's face profusely.

"Come now, Maranda, seeing you like this is not good for her. Let's leave her to sleep. She needs all the rest she can get." Dr. Greg led Maranda to the door. "I have to go now, but don't hesitate to call if you need anything, okay."

"Holy crap!" Remembering Emma and Logan, Maranda ran down the hospital corridor towards the I.C.U. again. (*And this day keeps getting better and better, she whispered sarcastically)*

CHAPTER EIGHTEEN

Maranda could feel an instant chill as she entered the room. "Logan..." Her feet dragged with heaviness.

He looked up, shaking his head. "It's over, Maranda. She's gone. She left us." his words were as emotionless as his eyes' blank look.

"What?" Needing to sit, she covered her face with shaking hands, collapsing into a chair.

"It can't be. This has to be just a bad dream, right?" his voice grew weak, staring at the floor.

"Oh, Hun," she rubbed his back with slow strokes.

"How could I not know, Maranda? She had been sick for months. How could she keep something as important as this from me, from us?"

"I know what she did may seem wrong in your eyes, but in her defense, I think she made the right decision by keeping this from you and the girls, Logan."

"How could you defend her? She rubbed us off the opportunity to be there for her. We could have spent more time together. We would not have left her side."

"And don't you see that's why she made the decision she did? It would have torn you to pieces, Logan, watching her slip away day after day, knowing there's nothing you or anybody could do about it."

"I would have been there for her, Maranda. She wouldn't have had to go through this alone."

"And do you think she would have wanted pity? I think Emma thought this thing through. She knew what would happen to her. Logan knew exactly how she wanted to live the rest of her life out, whatever little was left of it, and at the same time, she wanted to do right by you and the girls. In my eyes, Logan, she died a hero."

Sagging back in his chair, his eyes filled with tears. "She did..." his voice broke into a sob.

Maranda rushed to her brother's side. "It's going to be okay, Logan. I promise to stay by your side every step of the way, Hun. We'll get through this together."

Too numb even to return Maranda's hug, Logan's hands hang loose to the side.

"Do you know what her last request of me was?" closing his eyes reliving their last moments together

"What?" Maranda sank to her knees. Her hands were resting on Logan's lap. And she looked up at him.

Taking a while before he started speaking again. "She asked that I get married to Caroline as soon as possible, said that she had already spoken to her about it, and she agreed." Letting out a pained expression, he passed a hand over his mouth. "She knew, Maranda, she knew all along. She also said I should expect exciting news in the coming weeks, revel in it, and not let her death get in the way of my and the girls' happiness."

"Oh, Logan. Did she, by any chance, say or hint as to what this news is about? "She did." clamping his fingers together, he folded his hands behind his head, leaning back. "Caroline is with child."

Maranda immediately pulled back, speechless.

"Yep," Logan got to his feet, pushing his hand into a side pocket and walking towards the wall. "She did mention that Caroline does not know this information, which makes me wonder..."

"I, how did she know then?" fumbling to form words

"Well, that's what I've been wondering," he said, Pulling out his cell phone.

"What are you doing? Who? Whom are you going to call?" Maranda could only hope the panic she felt inside did not convey in her voice, taking the phone from Logan's hand.

"I should call Caroline to let her know what's happening here. I owe her that at the very least."

"You owe her nothing. Right now, you need to focus on the situation, which is making the funeral arrangements and whatever the hell one does under these circumstances. You don't need anything side-tracking you now; there will be plenty of time for that later. This needs your undivided attention. The girls need your full attention." not wanting to sound too harsh. "I will speak to Caroline. I'll ask her to give you the time you need. I'm sure under the circumstances, she'll understand."

"Yes, yes, I guess you're right."

That was a close call. Maranda breathed a sigh of relief. The last thing Logan needs right now is any more added stress. He'll tear John to pieces should he come to find out.

She could see it now, the full brunt of his anger unleashing. They would probably have to be making funeral arrangements for two. This she was pretty sure of, for when Logan was finished with John, not even hell would accept him as the son of a bitch.

"I'm looking for a Miss. Maranda Forrester." The uniformed Police enquired, "I was told by Dr. Wheeler I can find her here."

"What do you want with her?" Logan spoke in a rough and defensive tone, sidestepping at Maranda's side.

"Well, I need some information on an incident that happened earlier today to one called..."

"I'm Maranda," stepping forward. "It's okay, Logan, just a minor accident. I'll handle it." she walked to the door, another close call. She wasn't quite sure how long she'd be able to keep this thing a secret from Logan, but she'd be grateful at least until after the funeral took place. "Could you just give me one minute, please? I'll be right out." informing the police.

"No problem, Mam," replying loudly but professionally.

Returning to the room, "Go home, Logan. You can do nothing else here. Besides, you have to tell the girls. You guys really should be together in this time of grief." Giving her brother a prolonged comforting hug. "There are a few loose ends I must tie up here before I leave. I'll drop by very early in the morning if you need to get yourself some rest. You look like crap. I'm here for you; always remember that, okay." Maranda watched her brother walk away with sagged shoulders.

"Do you mind if we talk here at the hospital, please? I really should be returning to my friend. I want to be by her side when she awakes."

"Yes, sure, I understand." The officer took his notepad out, walking with Maranda towards Caroline's room. "Dr. Wheeler informed me about your family's loss. Please accept my condolences."

"Thanks."

CHAPTER NINETEEN

Logan closed the front door, exhaling an audible breath.

That was the last of the guests, and the kids were safely tucked in bed, fast asleep. The funeral service for Emma went as well as can be expected, considering it was a funeral. He can safely say he was numb for most of it.

People came and went, offering their condolences, shaking hands, hugging, crying, and offering their silent prayers. Logan was utterly blank throughout it all, breathing a sigh of relief that it was finally over.

Maybe now he'll be able to rest without a million and one phone calls bombarded with friends and loved ones offering their sympathies in this time of grief. Yes, he knew their hearts were in the right place, but he would appreciate some peace, quiet, and normalcy back into his life now.

Pouring a glass of whiskey, he took a mouthful as his eyes roamed around the room. He could almost feel the emptiness in the house. Taking another drink, he walked over to the balcony.

Maranda propped herself against the doorway with folded arms. "Hey."

"Hey," Logan replied without turning

"How's it going?"

Taking a sip of whiskey. "It's going." With a pained expression, he focused on the sky. "What can I say." he lifted his shoulders. "Life goes on, right?"

"It has to, Hun." Maranda closed the gap between them, hugging herself

"Yes, it does, and that's the sad part. I wonder if she's up there, looking down on us, the girls." He pointed to the sky with his drink in hand and a blank look on his face.

Maranda looked up at the sky. "I'm sure she is."

"You know I can't help but think of Emma's last request, her dying wish." He turned to Maranda, a strained look covering his face. "Have you spoken to Caroline?"

Maranda lowered her head, feeling a pinch of guilt. "No, I haven't."

Logan walked indoors. "Do you, by any chance, know where my cell phone is?"

"Why don't you get yourself some rest, Logan? You can always call Caroline in the morning," following behind him.

"With all that's been taking place, I completely forgot about her." he scampered around. "Where the fuck is my cell phone? Well, will you help me find it?" he said, raising his voice. "Never mind." grabbing the landline, he dialed Caroline's number. "That's funny." He placed the receiver down slowly before quickly picking it up and redialing. "Her phone is going straight to voicemail." He turned to Maranda, his eyebrows drawn close together. Once again, he places the receiver down, repeating the process.

"She's not going to pick up." Maranda's voice was soft and uncertain, realizing she could no longer keep this from Logan.

"What did you say?"

"Caroline is not going to answer the phone, Logan." She answered with a shaky voice

Placing the phone down, Logan ambled toward Maranda, feeling a sudden tightness in his chest. "And why would she not answer?"

At this point, Maranda froze. A heavy, sinking feeling took over her stomach. Not knowing what or how to tell Logan, she turned away. Feeling Logan's eyes piercing through her back, she started to shake.

"Tell me!" Logan shouted

Maranda burst into tears when her eyes met Logan's.

Logan's hand reached out, grasping her shoulders. "Where is Caroline, Maranda!" He shook her.

"She's in the hospital, Logan."

Logan's eyes widen. "Hospital, what is she doing in a hospital?"

"I think you should sit down for what I'm about to tell you." Maranda retreated to a chair. Her knees were much too weak to hold her up for much longer.

"You don't need to tell me; I think I can figure this out alone." He walked to the bar, getting himself another glass of whiskey. "Emma was right about Caroline being pregnant, wasn't she?" he waited for Maranda's response.

"Yes, she was."

"And let me take another wild guess. She had a miscarriage?"

"Yes, she did." once again, her response was short.

Logan lowered his gaze. "How did she take it? My God, I should have been there to support her."

"She doesn't know yet, Logan." Maranda looked up at him, still finding difficulty in saying the words.

"What do you mean she doesn't know what is going on here, Maranda, and why do I get the feeling that you're keeping something from me?"

"It's because I am. You have to understand, Logan. Emma had just passed, and things happened so fast I didn't know what to do." Her eyes met his, bringing her tone to a much lower one. "So, I did the only thing I thought was right then."

"That day you called at the hospital wasn't about Emma, was it?"

"No, they had just bought Caroline in."

"But I don't understand that was four days ago. Why is Caroline still in the hospital?" he stared at Maranda, unsure he wanted the answer.

"There's more,"

"Figured that much, given your reaction."

Maranda got to her feet. "John went over to the house that evening, Logan." She shook her head, for even as the words left her lips, she found it hard to believe. "By the time I'd gotten to her, she was already beaten to a slump."

Logan's hands instantly formed into a fist, not quite believing the words as they left his sister's mouth. "Her injuries, how bad?" His stony expression was that of a man who is ready to kill.

"Barely alive, she lost so much blood. The knife barely missed her spine, Logan."

"Knife?" Logan sank to the couch in a state of disbelief.

"There's more, Logan,"

Rubbing his hand over his face, he looked up, bracing himself.

"The doctors had predicted that Caroline would have been up and about by now," tears streamed down her cheek once again, shaking her head from side to side. "She hasn't woken up since that day, Logan."

Logan could feel the blood rushing through his veins, and his pulse racing thrummed against his forehead.

"They said there isn't anything more they could do for her at this stage, so it's a wait-and-see game for now."

"That's why the police were there that night?"

Maranda nodded

"John, is he in custody?"

"No, he's been in hiding since. No one has seen or heard from him since that night."

In a feverish haste, Logan grabbed his jacket and headed for the door. "Stay with the girls, Maranda."

"Where are you going?" he rushed out the door, disregarding Maranda. "Logan, please don't go getting yourself into any trouble."

Her voice died down. Standing in the doorway, she watched Logan's van pull out of the driveway and onto the road, exceeding the speed limit.

"Look who finally decided to show his face. Took you long enough." John got up and walked
over to the refrigerator, holding a beer out to Logan. "Care to have one? I can't say I wasn't expecting you." Placing the beer in his mouth. "Oh, where are my manners? Please accept my sympathies." He sat down, kicking a chair across the room to Logan, crossing his legs on the table. "Please have a seat." Sliding a beer to the opposite side of the table, "Let's drink to us single guys. you're already there, and I, well... word on the streets is I'll be there soon too." His contemptuous remark was meant to provoke Logan

Logan stoned: cold, silent glare fixed on John as he took his jacket off, throwing it across the chair. He began rolling his sleeves up, cracking his neck from side to side. He rubbed his wrists together.

"Come on now, don't tell me you're going to let a bitch come in between our friendship, Logan. Just look at it this way: You took my woman away. I just returned the favor. It's like a tit-for-tat situation." he grinned. "Let's say we call it even," he continued to bait Logan.

"Get to your feet." Punching John in the face with full force, Logan pulled back just long enough for John to climb back to his feet again. "You like hitting women, don't you?" Let's see how it feels when the tables are turned, and you're at the other end." Clenching his jaw, Logan's fist thwacked out again, with all the built-up rage inside, throwing John halfway across the room. "Come on," Logan called out to John. "Get up. It's time you pick on someone your size."

John climbs back to his feet, staggering. "Was she that good of a fuck, Logan?" He held on to the wall for support, wiping his nose. He glanced at the blood on his hand.

Striking John several times, Logan stood over him, dealing him two strikes with his foot in the back. "John, yes, she was." Picking his jacket, Logan strikes him one last time. “This one is for my unborn child.” Logan walks towards the door.

“Don’t tell me you’re finished, and you hit like a girl Logan.” John stood holding his stomach, staggering back and forth as he leaned against the wall.

Logan stared at Clair as she stood blocking the doorway's entrance.

“Bet you don’t feel so high and mighty now, Logan?” John burst out laughing. “That’s my girl, exactly like we planned it, okay,” he ordered Clair.

With shaking hands Clair, she pointed the gun at Logan. “You will never lay your hand on me or any other woman again. Turning the gun to John, she fired, watching him crumble to the floor. She fell to her knees, crying.

Logan listened to the sound of sirens drawing closer. He threw his jacket over his shoulder and left the house, finding his way to the hospital.

“Hey, you’re finally up. I was beginning to think you were never going to wake up.” Logan stroked Caroline’s cheek

A faint smile curved her lips. “No such luck. You’re not getting rid of me that easily.” She barely whispered, grimacing in pain.

“That’s my girl.” Logan laughed, gently kissing her forehead. “I love you, Caroline. I promise no one is ever going to come between us again. Today marks a new beginning to the rest of our life together.”

www.ingramcontent.com/pod-product-compliance
Lightning Source LLC
LaVergne TN
LVHW050556160826
845677LV00011B/2342

* 9 7 8 9 7 6 9 7 2 7 1 1 3 *